OUT OF NOWHERE

BECA LEWIS

PERCEPTION PUBLISHING

CONTENTS

PROLOGUE

Years passed before she told anyone what happened—years before there was someone in her life who might believe her.

At first, she didn't accept it herself. Instead, Maya Jade Maguire told herself she was dreaming. Told herself she had fallen asleep for a moment with the sun beating down, and the grass smelling so sweet beneath her.

But every slow-motion beat of time remained burned in her brain. And even though Maya sometimes wished she had been dreaming, most of the time she remained grateful for that magical moment and what came after.

What made it even more astonishing was the silence. Later, Maya would wonder why there was not a ripping sound in the universe. Something. Perhaps lightning and thunder. A darkening of the sky.

But nothing like that happened. No sound. It was an ordinary fall day filled with the smell of crushed leaves and fireplaces. That day, like many before, she had escaped the house and the drama that lay within and come to her favorite place in the park where they let the grass grow into a meadow that rippled in the wind.

It was where she would spend hours imagining shapes in the clouds and daydream. They were dreams of a teenager, yearning to be free of the life she had been born into. She wanted something more.

She daydreamed about fantastical worlds with magical beings, so at first, what she saw didn't surprise her. And then it did.

Which is why even now, all these years later, she still wondered if she had hallucinated or dreamed what occurred that day. But a daydream wouldn't explain her life.

When she finally dared to ask him where he had come from, he said, "Nowhere."

"How can you come from nowhere?" she asked.

He had only smiled at her.

"Okay," she said. "So if you are telling the truth, how did you get here?"

His face grew serious, and he paused before answering.

"I fell."

The way he said it made her wonder if perhaps he hadn't fallen. Maybe he had not told her the whole story. But she didn't want to know more. Maya was too happy he was in her life.

Much later, when he asked if she wanted to live with him in the place he called Nowhere, she said, "Yes." And he obliged.

ONE

The tree spread above Pax, shifting in the breeze, each limb stark against the dark blue sky—pale sunlight sifting through spring green leaves not yet fully unfurled threw shadows against the clouds that lay below.

In the distance, the hoot of an owl reminded him of his grandfather, Akotas, who had taught him the calls of the birds. So he hooted back, his best imitation of the owl he could muster, which wasn't very good.

His heart wasn't in it. It was only out of habit that Pax answered the owl, a habit formed from years of training. That is what his people did. If you hear a bird call, return the greeting.

But this owl was too far away to hear his tiny bleated response. He doubted the owl would have heard him, even if it had been sitting on a limb a few feet from him. It didn't matter in the least. He didn't want the owl to come to him, at least not now.

"Sorry, grandfather," he whispered, although he understood his grandfather would never hear him. Besides, he didn't have to say he was sorry. Pax knew if his grandfather could, he would pat him on the shoulder and tell him it was okay. But it wasn't okay, and his grandfather would not be patting him on his shoulder. Akotas had moved on, his duty done.

Akotas had stayed long past his time to depart, which only added to Pax's list of things he felt guilty about. His grandfather had tried to make up to Pax for a missing mother and father. He spent years attempting to turn Pax into someone the people in Crann could look up to as they looked up to Akotas, refusing to admit that it was a losing cause.

Akotas had never shown his discouragement that his son's son was not living up to the requirements of the Decana clan. At least he attempted never to show it. Instead, lesson after lesson, he would smile and say, "Try again, my heart."

Eventually, Pax learned the basics of what he was supposed to know. At least enough not to embarrass his grandfather during the annual testing of the children of the Decana. Although Pax would come in last in every event, at least he finished. It was better than the many years when he had failed at everything, and the people of the clan would turn their back on him, pretending he didn't exist.

Only his grandfather continued to provide Pax with love, his eyes filled with kindness and support, never with disappointment. It was one of his grandfather's greatest gifts. Not only his expansive heart and personal strength, but his ability to mask his true feelings in order to teach.

Because his grandfather didn't teach only Pax; he was the clan's teacher, a leader of the people with his sister, Isira. Akotas didn't need the yellow and orange markings on his cheekbones to tell people what he was. Every movement, every sound, every glance, was a teaching moment for anyone watching.

Akotas failed only twice. No one said so, but everyone knew. First, he had failed his son, and now his grandson.

Akotas' son failed in a fight with the Satoka, fighting until the end, his wife beside him, using every power of his people. But it hadn't been enough.

Pax knew the story. They had left him safe in the trees, hidden within the cavity of a massive white oak. His grandfather found him after the battle. Holding tight to his grandfather, Pax had seen the tears on his face and felt the wound in his grandfather's heart, broken in half because he had failed. Failed as a teacher, failed as a father.

Pax knew what Akotas had vowed that day: never to fail again. Knowing what people were thinking was one of his gifts, although it didn't feel like a gift to Pax. This gift pained him every moment of the day and night. This gift was one he would give back for any of the other skills that the members of his clan had, because theirs were useful. They could fight. He could not.

This gift of his was useless. It never served him, only punished him. Because that day, even as a small child, he saw the truth about the pain and disappointment his grandfather felt and felt it with him. Hearing what people didn't say or want others to know didn't bring him happiness, only confusion.

It was why he was alone, here on this small cloud caught between the boughs of the Tree of Life. Alone, he only felt his own thoughts, and that was hard enough.

But Pax understood the time would come when he would have to come down from the tree, but without the person who knew and loved him the best. He had only one thing going for him. It was the last thing his grandfather gave him.

Even now, Pax could play back every word his grandfather had said that day.

"My heart. I see you as you are. I always have."

With those words, his grandfather had opened a piece of himself Pax had never seen. And at that moment, Pax became a man. Not a teacher like his grandfather. Not a warrior, like his parents. Something else.

What that was, he didn't know. Yet. But Pax embraced the knowledge that he had been seen and accepted. Once. Perhaps that was enough to withstand what was coming.

Sighing, Pax let the cloud fold around him. He had seen caterpillars hanging from tree limbs within their crystal sacks, and the thought drifted through his mind that it was what he might look like to someone who could see him.

But no one could. Pax had two gifts. At least one of them might be useful.

TWO

B efore...

Akotas and Dradon stood together on the cliff that overlooked the three rivers that lay below them.

Their sister, Isira, stood near them, the morning sun behind her, the wind lifting tiny curls from the long thick braid of dark hair that hung down her back, looking like the High Priestess she was born to be.

Three paths, Akotas thought, *just like them.* Except the three rivers merged into one. That the three of them could become of one mind was impossible.

They had met at the cliff because their parents had died, and this is where every generation before them had stood before assuming leadership of their clan, the Decana.

Because first, before their responsibilities began, they were granted two full moons of freedom to grieve and explore. They would meet again after their last alone time was over.

When they returned, Isira would replace their mother as the High Priestess. It was a role Isira had trained for all of her life. One of her duties would be to lead the council of women. The council would decide what was best for their clan. The men carried out their wishes. It had worked well for countless generations.

If things had been normal, Akotas and Dradon would replace their father. They would divide the tasks of protecting and feeding their people and supporting Isira. That was their duty. But all three of them were fully aware it would not work that way. All because of Dradon. Dradon had no desire to share anything.

Isira accepted that sometimes a ruler who demanded more power could be something the people needed. In the past, that kind of ruler would arrive in time to move the people forward, force them to think differently to prepare them to thrive in a changing future. Isira understood a forceful ruler came along only when a clan would not survive unless someone took over for a time. And she knew a ruler who insisted on progress sometimes had to rule alone and by his own rules. But it was never for themselves. It was for the good of the clan.

But Dradon's need for power was not for the good of the clan. He did not care to move their people forward. He wanted all the power for himself. For him there was no other purpose. People could live or die, and Dradon felt nothing.

All Dradon ever desired was the ability to make people do what he wanted them to do. His desire for power became clear almost immediately. Yes, when they were very young children, there were fleeting moments of laugher and getting along, but mostly Dradon punched, pulled, and bullied.

Was he made that way on purpose? Isira often asked herself. Why would society need someone like her brother? Was this a mistake or something planned? Isira never went past the question of how or why something might be pre-ordained. Did it matter what or who planned their destiny? What mattered is what they did about it.

As a child, Isira did her best to stay out of Dradon's way. She and Akotas had often been the recipients of Dradon's cruelty and need to rule everyone and everything. It brought the two of them closer and strengthened them. But eventually, Dradon's cruelty became too much for everyone to ignore. And even though he was the son of the High Priestess, what he did and how he acted needed to stop.

Finally, their parents could no longer deny that their son had been born with what the clan considered a disease. They waited as long as possible to do something about it. The village tried to cure him of his cruel ways. But Dradon did not become better. Instead, everything they did only increased his abilities as he fought their influence. Dradon's cruelty and single-mindedness to rule over everyone and everything grew. Finally, the village, their parents, and the women's council accepted that Dradon could not remain within the clan, and they banished him.

Isira and Akotas knew the banishment broke their parent's hearts. But as the ones in charge of the clan's welfare, they could not let him stay. They knew the disease their son carried could, and would, spread throughout the clan, destroying the peace they had enjoyed for generations.

After they banished Dradon, the village burned everything of his in a fire, erasing his existence. Isira knew her parents secretly hoped he survived, but for the welfare of the people, they needed him to die in the wilderness.

Peace returned to the village and their family. Isira and Akotas concentrated on learning about their future roles, and almost forgot they once had a brother. But eventually news came of a new clan of people. The Satoka. A clan filled with people who fought and killed and did not live with the land. That was when they all knew Dradon had not died in the wilderness, but had thrived. And was doing what they were afraid he would do. Disrupting the peace.

And now Dradon stood before them. Grown. His face hard.

Dradon had heard of their parent's passing, and as was the tradition, had come to this cliff on the sixth day of mourning to acknowledge their passing and to accept responsibility to take care of their people.

Except Dradon said he was the ruler of both clans now. His clan, the Satoka, and the Decana. He would let Akotas and Isira be the figureheads of the Decana, but he would be the actual ruler. All they needed to do was agree to do what he demanded.

However, he would give them time to decide what they would do. They would keep the tradition of a time of freedom after a parent's passing before they took their place in the clan. Perhaps they would decide not to rule and leave all the clans to him.

"You know we cannot do that, Dradon. We can't let you divide and rule the people with cruelty," Akotas said.

"Well, then perhaps you should use your freedom to find a way to stop me," Dradon smirked. "It wouldn't be fun to destroy you now, anyway. You would be helpless. So I promise to let the Decana alone for the next two full moons.

"But you should know that the desire to punish these people for banishing me and hoping I would die in the wilderness burns within me. I wake at night and see the village in flames. Women and children screaming. Men laying flayed before me. That vision has fueled me for years. But surprising you would have been too easy. I want and need a fight.

"But since you are my siblings, I have given you the other option. I won't destroy the village in that way. But I will rule it. And you will follow my orders.

"This is the only way the village remains. Otherwise, everyone in it dies. The two of you will be last. You will watch them suffer before I fight you both to the death—one at a time. And you know I will win. So choose well my brother and sister."

As Akotas listened, he felt a fire rising inside of him. Years of enduring his brother's bullying and cruelty filled his head. He saw again all the suffering Dradon inflicted on everyone around him.

Akotas' anger exploded, and without thinking, he grabbed Dradon and wrestled him to the ground.

Dradon only laughed and despite knowing this was what Dradon wanted, and he had fallen into the trap, Akotas couldn't get out of it.

Dradon pulled one arm free from Akotas' grip and started punching Akotas in the face, laughing harder each time he drew blood.

Isira screamed at them to stop. Neither one of them listened to her.

As the two men wrestled, Akotas locked his body around Dradon, Dradon screeching with laughter. Neither of them noticed they were rolling closer and closer to the edge of the cliff. What happened next changed everything. Not just for them, but for the other world they fell into.

THREE

Isira screamed, reached for Akotas, her fingertips grazing the edge of his shirt as he and Dradon fell off the cliff and vanished. She was still screaming, kneeling at the edge of the cliff, when the red-tailed hawk known as Koda streaked past her and dived after them.

A second later, a second hawk landed beside Isira, screaming too, feeling the same pain. Both of them had just witnessed the ones they loved falling into the Nowhere. Ceya, the hawk, wanted to follow her mate Koda, her feet stamping at the edge of the cliff, raising little puffs of dirt, feathers ruffling in the wind, wings opening and closing, preparing to fly. Wherever Koda went, she wanted to go, too. But she couldn't. Her duty was to Isira's family. It was Koda's duty too, which is why he hadn't hesitated.

Ceya suspected Koda had not stopped for a second to consider any other course of action. He came from a long line of hawks who watched over and protected the family that guided the Decana clan, so Koda would follow the brothers over the cliff, no matter the cost to him.

Isira stopped screaming when she realized someone needed to get her brothers and bring them home, and she was the only person who could do it.

That the cliff was an opening into another world was something the leaders of the Decana knew. It was a story passed down to them through their parents. Long ago, a man climbed the cliff and stepped into the land of the Decana. That he climbed the cliff was considered impossible, and when he claimed he did, her people, lawless then and often cruel, threw him over it.

Everything that had fallen, or that they threw over the cliff, always disappeared within seconds. The same thing happened with the cliff-climbing man. He disappeared that day, but returned the next. Eventually, they tired of throwing him over the cliff and decided he must be a god.

The man said that he wasn't a god at all. He only wanted to help them find peace. He had appeared out of nowhere and when asked where he came from, that was his answer: "I come from Nowhere."

He said his name was William, but they called him William Sky because he had climbed into the sky to find them. What was important, he said, was that the people of the world they called Crann become peaceful, and that was why he was there.

Acceptance and then peace were a long time coming, but eventually, people listened, and the children of the men who threw him over the cliff became devoted to his ideas. William Sky brought peace to all the people that lived near the three rivers. And that peace eventually spread throughout all of Crann. Then he helped them form traditions and rules that would maintain that peace.

Only then, after appointing a family to guide the Decana, who in turn guided the people of Crann, did he tell that family the magic of the cliff. He warned them never to throw things over it again. It disrupted another world. To make sure that didn't happen, William showed the family how to keep the cliff edge invisible to others. He said he had done the same to the base of the cliff. In this way, both worlds would be safe from each other.

After everything was in place, William Sky said goodbye, and the leaders of the Decana watched him step off the cliff. No one in Crann ever saw him again.

So when Isira watched Dradon and Akotas fall, she knew where they had gone. They had fallen into the world of William Sky.

Isira had seen the two of them separate as they fell, which meant they didn't end up in the same place. And yet, she needed to find them both and bring them back. She couldn't imagine the horror that Dradon might inflict on the unwitting people he would meet, and without Akotas, she did not believe she could rule effectively.

Isira dropped her head to the ground and prayed she would do the right thing. Should she go after Akotas or after Dradon? And because she had hesitated before following them, they would not be exactly where they landed. Each moment that passed made finding them more difficult.

Finally, Isira decided. She would follow Akotas. Perhaps between the two of them, they would find Dradon. She hoped she could persuade her brothers to return before the two full moons took place.

Isira knew the cliff would be invisible to her once she was in the other world. William Sky had explained that if something happened, the only way to find the cliff again was to leave part of themselves behind.

Taking the knife she always wore on her belt, Isira reached behind her for her long braid and hacked it off at her neck. What she wanted to do was howl with sorrow at what she was losing and scream with anger at the two men who had caused this problem. Instead, she lifted her face again to the sun, feeling its warmth, and wondered if it was the same sun she would find in the other world.

Ceya plucked a feather from her wing and dropped it on the ground in front of her.

"Thank you, Ceya. Yes, please come with me."

Isira took her hair and the feather and placed them carefully in a deep hollow of the oak tree that lived near the cliff's edge. The wind caressed her exposed neck as she took one last look behind her, breathed in the sweet air filled with the scent of early lilacs, lifted her face to the sun, and asked it to lead her and her brothers back safely to this world. Yes, even Dradon. She would deal with him when they returned.

Replaying the direction of Akotas' fall in her mind, she stepped off the cliff. Ceya followed her, folding her wings as she dived, neither of them knowing what they would find or if they would be safe where they were going.

FOUR

Now...

Ginny Ariana Maguire heard the day beginning. It was hard to miss. Downstairs her mother clanged pots and dishes and complained to herself, like a mantra that she repeated over and over again, not realizing that she was doing it.

The sun wasn't up yet, but the two of them were, as always. Ginny knew that if she lay in bed a little longer, the yelling and clanging would stop, then the door would slam as her mother left for work.

It was tempting. She could let her mother head off for the day without her. She could stay in bed where it was warm. The bedroom was freezing. Her mother didn't heat the house no matter how cold it got. It kept their expenses down.

Everything was about keeping expenses down and earning enough money to not end up in the street. "That is something that will never happen," her mother would yell. "Never. As long as I have breath in my body, we will have a house."

Ginny sighed. She knew she should be grateful for a mother that worked to keep them fed and housed even if it was cold, and what waited downstairs for her was not something she wanted to eat. She wanted to stay in bed and go back to the dream where she and her mother were not poor. Back to the times when they would snuggle in bed together and read, or her mother would put the book down and tell her stories instead. When her mother would tuck her under her arm, kiss her on the forehead, and tell her stories of magical people and cheerful places.

As her mother talked, Ginny would let herself drift into the story until the story became as real to her as the home they lived in. Those times had stopped years before. Now her mother was no longer the beautiful light-on-her-feet woman with sun-tipped brown hair that fell in soft folds around her face. No longer was her face open and bright, so bright that everyone felt as if the sun was smiling on them.

That woman was long gone. Now her mother was hard and thin. Her hair no longer soft but pulled back so harshly it looked as if it would pop off her scalp. Her mother's sunshine smile was replaced with a scowl, little lines radiating out from her pursed lips.

The stories her mother had told no longer seemed real. They were fairy tales. And as Ginny reminded herself, not someplace to live. It was time to get up. She had to go to work. She had a class to teach. And she needed to say goodbye to her mother before she left. Perhaps today she could coax a small smile, or maybe her mother would let herself relax in her arms as Ginny hugged her goodbye.

There is always hope, Ginny told herself as she dragged herself out of bed. Even through the socks she kept on her feet at night in a vain attempt to stay warm, she felt the freezing floorboards as her feet hit the floor.

It wasn't that cold outside. How their house could always be as cold as if they lived in the Arctic was a mystery to Ginny. But she long ago gave up asking, because her mother would answer, "That's how it is." If she answered, which she rarely did.

Seeing her mother already at the door, Ginny hurried the last few steps to get to her before she turned the doorknob.

Her mother froze at her touch. It was like holding a piece of iron, but no longer straight. A curved bow strung so tight sometimes Ginny was afraid that it would snap and send them both flying against the wall.

"Mom," Ginny said, laying her head on her mother's rigid back.

"I have to go," her mother whispered through clenched teeth.

Ginny backed up so her mother could open the door. For a moment, she thought she saw her mother's fingers tremble on the doorknob, and then she was out the door, shutting it behind her, leaving Ginny staring at it.

Not for the first time, Ginny wondered how a door could become so ugly. Was it always this ugly? Didn't she have a memory of a lovely door, the wood so brightly polished it shone?

If her mother would talk about it, Ginny was sure she would say it had always looked this way. But did it? And if it looked beautiful before, why did it look like this now? The door was another version of her mother. Gray, battered, tense, barely working.

Ginny turned and glimpsed herself in the hall mirror. The mirror freaked her out. Something about it made her uneasy, as if it watched her. But if Ginny was anything, she was practical, and she knew that wasn't possible. Mirrors did not have eyes, so she had long ago decided she didn't like it because it was so hard to see into it. It wasn't practical. Why keep a cloudy, scratched, and cracked mirror?

Once, she tried to take it off the wall. And couldn't. It was stuck. When her mother caught sight of her trying to remove it, she screamed at her to stop.

"But it's a terrible mirror, mom. Let me get a new one and put it here."

Trembling, her hand on the wall, her mother answered so softly that Ginny barely understood her.

"No, it was your father's. Leave it."

It was the first time she had heard her mother even say she had a father. She wanted to shake her and demand to know what she meant. But her mother had gathered her strength and given her a look that told her there would be no more.

She could not move the mirror. She would not learn more about a father. That was final.

And like all things in her life, Ginny resigned herself to it. As much as she wanted it to be different, this was how it was.

Today, the mirror remained as cracked and cloudy as always. But for a second, perhaps because a ray of light struck its surface, Ginny saw herself: wrapped in a robe, bunny slippers that somehow escaped the ruthlessness of her mother removing anything cute from the house, wild dark hair curling into space as if it had a mind of its own, and confused gray eyes that seemed too large for her face even now as a grown woman.

As a child, they earned her the name "bug eyes." She had pretended to like the name so they would stop teasing her. It had worked. It was a small, essential skill she had learned from a frozen mother. Never let them see how she really felt. She often wondered if she remembered anything that was true, because now it seemed she did not know how she felt about anything anymore.

She, like her mother, needed to get to work. And because a sense of duty was something she understood, that was what she would do. Besides, being in a room full of six-year-olds forced her out of her current life and into theirs. Their lives were full of promise and potential, or should be. So even if she couldn't do that for herself, she could see it for them.

FIVE

Everything about life was painful to Maya Jade Maguire. But the pain of keeping her daughter Ginny away from her had long passed from pain to torture to numbness, an almost exquisite numbness where she felt, saw, and knew nothing. All she needed to do each day was her job and stay silent. That doing so removed her from everything that brought light and joy didn't matter. What mattered was Ginny was safe and would remain safe as long as she kept her promise.

To stay sane, Maya had to believe Dradon would keep his promise as long as she kept hers. However, sometimes Maya wondered if it would be easier if she let herself die. Maya knew a way to accomplish it, a way that made an unsuspicious death possible. Because if she died, perhaps Ginny would be of no use to Dradon because Ginny knew nothing about the secret. Yes, Ginny would be without a mother or father, but at least she would be free.

But Dradon told Maya that if she died on purpose, it broke the agreement, and all hell would break loose. Dradon wasn't making an idle threat. He could do it. Dradon, her husband's brother, Ginny's uncle, was a powerful man. So instead of dying, she would remain silent and hold on to the tiny flame of hope that someone would come and help them before Dradon came to collect what he said belonged to him.

The good car was in the garage for Ginny. Maya's car sat outside on the cracked driveway where weeds grew with abandon. It wouldn't have mattered if they had a place to put her car. It would look like this, anyway. The car had once been beautiful, like the house, but now it wasn't. Rusted, decayed, and barely running. Again, just like her.

Backing out of the driveway in her battered car, Maya looked at their house. She knew that children in the neighborhood called it the haunted house. Maya acknowledged that's what it looked like. And she was glad. In fact, she helped it along. A large weeping willow obscured the upstairs window, and when the wind blew a certain way, its long trailing branches lashed against the window, making unworldly screeching sounds.

Enormous untrimmed bushes grew past the porch railing and over the front steps, making it hard to get up them, and only the very determined bothered to try. The only person who found it easy was the mail carrier. Maya made sure they always found the safe route up the stairs because they might be the one carrying a message that would change their lives.

Bats swooped at night, and the guttural sounds and hissing of cats deep in the bushes added to the haunted house aura. She didn't need to do any of that. The house invited them, and they stayed. In its own way, the house protected her and Ginny. Once, she had been profoundly grateful for their home's beauty and warmth. Now she had a smidgen of gratitude for its ugliness. It kept people away.

Especially the children. The scared ones crossed the street instead of walking past it. The ones who believed bravery and courage involved taunting and bullying threw rocks at the windows and yelled words from the shadows that Maya thought no one would use, let alone a child.

But even though she couldn't save the house from the look it took on when she made that promise, she could protect it and Ginny from harm. So the rocks bounced off the windows or disappeared before reaching them, and the words vanished within inches of the mouth of the person who yelled them.

That this caused more fear of the house was a good thing. It kept people away. Except for people who came with their instruments, standing as close as possible to measure what they believed could be measured. Everyone wanted an explanation of why the house looked that way, and why one woman who lived there looked like death being held up by wires, and another moved like a leaf in the wind and smiled like the sun.

Maya had walked across what passed as a yard to get to the car. A pot of mint she planted years before had long ago tipped over and then spread its roots throughout the small space. As Maya shuffled through it, barely lifting her feet, the mint sent its fragrance into the air. She couldn't smell it because she didn't want to. She only allowed herself one moment every morning as she sat still in her car to feel her forever abiding love for her daughter and her husband. He was long gone into another world. She sent a small silent prayer for Akotas' safety and then closed her heart again, locking it so nothing could slip in or out and ruin everything.

It was why she could not speak. Could not let Ginny hug her. She could not open any door that might invite Dradon into Ginny's life.

• • • • •• • • • • • •

Ginny's drive to work was terrible. It always was. The only good part about the stop-and-go traffic was that it gave her time to transition between the house and her mother and work life. It was as if she and her mother lived in one world, and everyone else lived in another.

The time in the car between these two worlds was a poor substitute for what she yearned for, but it enabled her to do her job and look like an ordinary person.

Well, I am an ordinary person, Ginny said to herself. *Except I can let no one meet my mother or see our house.*

Even when she was growing up, she went to her friends' houses. They never came to hers. Her mother did her best to appear normal when she had to go to the school to talk to her teachers, but afterward, Ginny always fielded questions about her mother's health.

Was her mother well? Was there anything they could do?

Once people came to their house to check on Ginny's welfare, but that day the house looked perfectly normal, and they left wondering why they had been called. For two weeks after that visit, her mother had been so ill Ginny almost called a doctor.

But her mother begged her to let it be. She was just tired and needed to rest. Maya got better, and no one ever came to the house again. Even then, Ginny lived in two worlds. The world of friends and school and the world of the house and her mother.

There is no use thinking about this, Ginny reminded herself. *This is my life. I might as well get used to it.*

And when she walked in the door of her classroom, and the children's faces smiled up at her, Ginny smiled back, figuring that it would have to be enough.

SIX

Maya didn't really have a job—at least not the type of job that Ginny assumed her mother was going to each morning. Maya had evaded Ginny's desire to visit her at work or learn what she did for so long that Ginny no longer asked.

Maya didn't need to work for money. Akotas had made sure she would always have enough, and neither Dradon nor Isira took that away from her. Dradon, because he knew she needed money to live, and Isira because they had once been friends. Maya snorted at the thought of the three siblings that became her family. Some family.

At least I have Ginny, Maya mused, as she maneuvered her rusted heap of a car through the traffic to where she would spend her day.

Maya drove away every morning to a job she didn't have, or need, to fool Ginny, so Ginny wouldn't worry. And, Maya admitted to herself, to give herself something to do other than sit alone in the house, too afraid to do anything other than hope Ginny would make a happy life for herself.

The trouble was, Ginny was not doing that. And now Maya worried her daughter would never make a life for herself because she believed she needed to take care of her sick mother.

Maya sighed. This life was not the life she once dreamed about. She once expected she would live a magic life. Well, it had magic, just not the magic Maya once wanted. But then, how could she have known?

She had been an ordinary girl living with normal parents who worked regular jobs until that day when Akotas arrived out of nowhere.

That day, Maya was angry as always at her parents and the boredom of her life. She had gone to her favorite place to ponder how to change her life. Something that would differ from the life that loomed in front of her. She wanted adventure, and that day she was desperate.

The fighting at home was terrible. Her studies at school bored her, and she was considering either dropping out or changing her major at the University to something like Greek Myths and Legends. Perhaps by learning about them, she would look at the world differently and then live a vicariously adventurous life.

However, Maya understood that either choice would upset her parents. She lived at home because they had barely scraped the money together to send her to college. She knew what they would say if she changed her major to something so impractical.

"How can you make money with that kind of education? We haven't worked our entire lives for you to do something that frivolous!"

"Well, why do they have these classes then?" she'd ask her parents. "They must be there for a reason."

"They are for rich people," her father would answer. "People like us don't study just for fun."

The last time she discussed this with her parents, she had hugged them both and thanked them for their advice, even though Maya realized she would not follow it. But she loved them for what they had done for her, and she hated that if she lived life her way, she would hurt their feelings and disappoint them.

But Maya didn't want to live an ordinary life doing ordinary things. She never had. She wanted to be unique and do something meaningful. What that was, Maya didn't know. But she knew she loved being outside and not inside a stuffy classroom with what she considered mindless busy work, everyone listening to someone droning on and on about useless information. She realized her parents believed going to the University would somehow produce a job that paid better money than their factory jobs, but Maya had seen the writing on the wall.

Not only would that not happen for most people in her class, but it definitely would not happen for her. She could never sit or stand in one place for long, let alone have someone tell her what to do. Whatever she did with her life, it was not where her current life was taking her.

That day, when adventure fell out of the sky, she had been more depressed than usual. How could she please her parents and still have a meaningful life?

Now, all these years later, as Maya pulled into the park where she spent her days, she snorted again. At herself this time. Once, a long time ago, she worried about becoming a nobody at a tedious job, and ended up being somebody with a terrifying life. However, Ginny was the result, and that was enough for her. But it wasn't enough for Ginny. Maya needed a way to set Ginny free.

Maya now understood how much her parents had loved her. They gave up their hopes and dreams to give her a better life. She did that now for Ginny. But like Maya, Ginny was not happy. And the entire reason she agreed to Dradon's terms was to make sure Ginny would have a happy, safe, and fulfilling life.

As she always did, Maya hid her car in the far reaches of the lot. She experienced a moment of happiness because it was a beautiful day in which to walk and think. Akotas had always told her she would find answers among the plants and trees. She believed him, but for years there were no answers at all—only a long bleak stretch of living in fear.

Perhaps it would be different today. Perhaps something would happen to change the tragedy of their lives.

As Maya lifted her small backpack out of the car, she noticed the park's groundkeeper on the other side of the parking lot. He had been there for as long as she had been coming to the park.

He never came close enough for them to talk. But he was always there, waiting for her and her car.

Even from a distance, she could see his dark red hair ruffle in the wind. But she knew he saw her better than she saw him. She raised her hand in a wave, and he waved back. She always felt safer knowing he was around.

More than once, she walked toward him to thank him for taking such good care of the park and watching over her. But he would always disappear before she got there. Finally, she realized he wanted to be left alone, so she only waved when she came and went from the park.

She understood the need to be left alone.

Stepping onto the path, her water bottle tucked into her pack, along with a few food bars, Maya headed for the meadow. She always went there. She didn't know what she expected to happen. Just because something happened once did not mean it would happen again. But what if it did? What if history repeated itself? Would it be a good thing or a bad thing?

Maya didn't actually expect anything to happen, and she wasn't sure she wanted it to. What she wanted was an idea that would free her and Ginny. And if not the two of them, at least her daughter.

Observing from the grove of trees, Koda saw Maya shoulder her pack and head towards the path that would lead her to the meadow. He knew why she went there, and he understood what she wanted. He wanted it to happen, too.

He yearned to return home, but he promised Isira and Akotas to watch over Maya since they couldn't. Watching over their family had been his family's' role for generations, and Ginny and Maya were family now, too. Still, if there were a way to return and be with Ceya again, he would do whatever it took to accomplish it. So as Maya prayed for a solution, he prayed too, as he always did.

Perhaps today was the day they both would get an answer.

SEVEN

Because of her first-graders, Ginny loved teaching most of the time. It pleased Ginny that she was the one who introduced them to the pleasures of learning. And because Ginny recognized how it felt to be different, she believed she understood how to help them adjust to days in a classroom and fitting in—but still be themselves. She wanted to show them how to make learning enjoyable for them even when the teaching was terrible, as it would be at least once in their lives. And she wanted to help them apply what they learned to thrive in what could often be a harsh world.

She hoped what she taught them would serve them throughout their school years and into the life that came after. If Ginny could, she would give them all a magic wand that would direct them through the maze of people who didn't see their uniqueness or didn't care. But since she didn't have a magic wand to give them, she wanted her students to have the wisdom and courage to withstand times of hardship. Ginny knew that even now, some of these young children lived lives almost too hard for them to bear.

She looked out over her classroom and thought how each of these children's lives was a precious gem, and it was her job to discover how to polish it and bring it to life. Every day that the children sat in her classroom, she tried to make life better for them. She brought food to school, tutored after school, and often picked up students who lived in cars and took them out to eat and sometimes to the movies.

She found other parents and teachers who were willing to go out of their way, and they, too, watched over the students. Even the children who looked like they came from a good home with plenty to eat were often suffering because they hid secrets about themselves, believing if people knew, they wouldn't be accepted.

Within this circle of caring parents and teachers, they treasured and nurtured each child. She started the circle three years before when she began teaching full time, and she and the other members continued to check on the welfare of those students as they moved through the grades. Ginny and her circle considered expanding their reach to the other children in the school but worried that they wouldn't understand or even like what they were doing because they had not been Ginny's students. If they told anyone, the authorities might step in and stop them.

So as much as she wanted to reach out to everyone, Ginny hoped the students she and her circle nurtured would bring awareness and kindness into the world, and that would help bring about a much-needed change.

Ginny knew what it felt like to be different. The kids she grew up with teased her because of her bug eyes, and because her mother looked like a witch, and their house looked haunted. That would have been bad enough, but Ginny also knew something was wrong with her. She never felt as if she belonged anywhere. When she shared the things she thought about, the teachers reported her to the principal, who went to her mother and said they thought Ginny might have a mental disorder.

Seriously, she mused. *A mental disorder.* But what she remembered most was what happened after the meeting with the principal. As soon as they were safely inside their house, her mother took her hand and, in a rare moment of affection, told Ginny she was right. Some things are not as they seem, and yes, there are other universes, other times, other dimensions, but most everyone didn't know that, and mostly they didn't want to know. And besides, they lived in this one, so it was best to adjust to what they couldn't change.

Even now, Ginny barely believed that they had that conversation. For a moment in time, her mother was an entirely different woman. A younger one. A woman full of wit and life. And then that woman vanished, and the old, private, withdrawn woman returned.

For many years, Ginny prayed to see that mother again. As she got older, she wondered if perhaps her mother was also not as she appeared to be, and that was what she had been saying, in a roundabout way.

So Ginny hid what she felt, what she thought, and who she wanted to be so she could get through school. And that was why she was now a teacher. Perhaps by knowing each child, she would be at least one person in their life who showed them that who they were was beautiful and unique, and then helped them thrive in such a strange and often cruel world.

Today she was concentrating on the small tow-headed boy who sat at the front of the room. He sat there because she put him there. Tommy hated sitting up front, but if he didn't, he would fall asleep or put his head on his desk to hide. She moved him to the front of the room, hoping it would help her figure out how to help him. He was withdrawn and angry. Nothing she did so far worked, but she hoped the field trip they were going on would bring a smile to his face.

She didn't want to fail with him as she was failing with her mother. Although Ginny yearned to live a fuller life, she knew she couldn't. Somehow she and her mother were trapped. But she didn't understand how or why, and her mother wouldn't tell her.

Besides, she knew her mother lied to her for her entire life. Her mother said she had a job. Ginny knew she didn't, yet somehow there was money. Maya stopped asking her mother where she went to work on the day she followed her instead of going to school. Seeing her mother drive to a park and get out and walk astonished Ginny, but still, she wasn't too worried. Perhaps her mother was only taking a day off from work.

But Ginny followed Maya repeatedly until she was positive her mother was going to the park every day. For weeks after that, Ginny debated if she should tell her mother she knew she was lying. She wanted to ask her what was going on. But she didn't. Instead, she asked about work and her mother grunted as she often did, which meant something like, "It's okay and don't bother me."

That's when a profound sadness settled into Ginny's heart. Ginny knew she was different, but after that, she recognized that everything about her life was a lie. It took all of her courage every morning to pass on to the children the idea that kindness and wisdom ruled the world, despite appearances, and how to overcome adversity when she couldn't even change her own life. All because of her mother and her secret. It worried Ginny. Perhaps she was wrong about life. Maybe life was a hell and one they could never leave.

Ginny shook her head. Letting herself think those things would never help these children. But the depression was eating away at her, and every day it got harder and harder to find the hope that things could get better.

She looked out over the sea of faces, almost all of them smiling back at her, excited about the field trip, and decided that she could do one more day. For them, if not for herself.

EIGHT

Pax dropped from the tree using a trick he learned from the spider. Holding on to one string of the cloud, he lowered himself silently to the ground. Ceya cracked an eye as Pax dropped past her home in the tree, blinked, and waited to see where he was going. She and Pax had a long history together, and if Pax was going somewhere, she had to go too.

During the night, Pax had struggled to make a decision. He could remain in the woods and pretend he didn't hear Isira calling for him. He could stay alone but safe and relatively happy in the forest. Or he could follow the call that began as a small whisper in his heart but was now a roar in his head.

And as much as he hated to admit it, he understood he could not continue to ignore it. He treasured his independence and his autonomy, but his grandfather told him he had not come into this world to be alone and hide in the woods.

Pax would never forget the day his grandfather told him what his mission would be in this lifetime. They were celebrating his eleventh birthday with a prayer to his mother and his father—the flames from the fire warm and soft, sending sparks of light into the air.

Akotas became quiet after the celebration, and Pax was preparing for bed when his grandfather cleared his throat. Pax sat down again, knowing his grandfather needed to tell him something. But what Akotas told him was not what he had expected.

"You're old enough to learn why you are here, Pax."

Pax wanted him to stop talking. He knew Akotas would tell him he would need to prepare to be a warrior.

Instead, his grandfather told him it was his duty and destiny to keep the peace in their world. That the threat that war would return was real, and Pax would help stop it.

Pax laughed, thinking Akotas was teasing him. His grandfather continued to sit, staring at the fire, the flames now dancing and flaring as if in response to such an absurd statement.

Even at eleven, Pax recognized his lack of ability as a fighter, so how could he stop a war and keep the peace? Years before, when Akotas tried to show him how to fight, Pax had sat on the ground and cried.

That day, Akotas walked away and left him there in the dirt, sobbing. When Akotas didn't return, Pax climbed the tree and hid away with the clouds. Two days later his grandfather came back, bringing food from the village, and told Pax to come down from the tree.

Pax refused. All he could think about was how his grandfather had left him. He could not trust Akotas again. When Pax remained in the tree, Akotas built a fire and sat before it, eating the food he had brought.

In the morning, when Pax still had not come down from the tree, his grandfather summoned a great wind that pushed Pax out of the branches, sending him crashing to the ground.

Akotas slowed his fall the last few feet, so Pax landed softly on his back, staring up at the tree, which he imagined was bending over and laughing at him for being so useless.

When he didn't move, his grandfather reached his hand down and pulled him up, brushed him off, and handed him a bowl of fruit and a small loaf of bread.

"Eat," he said.

Pax wanted to pout. He wanted to turn around and run away, but he was so hungry he decided to eat first. He kept his head down as he stuffed the food in his mouth. When he finished, he set the bowl down, crossed his arms over his chest, and finally looked up at his grandfather.

Akotas was waiting, his dark brown eyes almost hidden within the folds of his face. A scar ran across his cheek, and as often as Pax asked him how he had gotten it, Akotas always replied, "It came to me when I wasn't looking."

Long moments passed, and Pax felt as if his grandfather was staring deep inside his soul. He made himself sit, telling himself that he was not useless and reminding himself that he had no one but his grandfather.

"I was wrong to walk away, Pax," Akotas said, and then added, "and you were wrong to react that way."

Pax closed in on himself, hugging his knees. All he heard was he was wrong to react that way. It wasn't until his grandfather said nothing more that he replayed what he heard and realized his grandfather said he was wrong, too.

Pax had nodded, and when his grandfather came to sit beside him, he leaned into him and sobbed. Akotas waited and when the sobbing stopped, Pax still felt afraid and still doubted, but something inside of him had strengthened. If his grandfather believed that about him, he was willing to admit that perhaps it was possible.

After that, his grandfather trained Pax differently. He told Pax he no longer expected him to be a warrior. There were other ways to lead and other ways to change the world. He no longer looked away when Pax closed in on himself and tried to disappear. Instead,

Akotas demanded that Pax come out of himself and let himself be seen.

When Pax would fold his arms in defiance, Akotas would give him a more challenging task to do. In time, Pax saw what Akotas was doing. He was accepting Pax as he was while demanding that he be more.

Wrapped in his cloud that night as he tried to decide what to do, Pax felt his grandfather's finger poking him in the chest the way he did before he left for good.

"I am in here, Pax. I will always be in here. You have a warrior's heart. You must do what you came here to do."

That morning, Pax had decided it was time to go out into the world and do what he came to do. Pax took his time preparing for the journey, knowing it might be the last time he would see these woods. It was no longer about what he wanted or how he wanted to live his life. It was time to do what needed to be done. Whether or not he wanted to was not the point. It was what he had to do.

He would go to Isira. He heard her calling. It was time to find out what she wanted.

Pax ducked into the large opening at the base of the tree and pulled out the woven bag his grandfather had left him. He had no possessions other than the bag. The forest was his home, and it had given him all that he needed. But Pax didn't want to leave the bag since Akotas gave it to him. Slipping it onto his back, something clunked against his spine.

Inside, he found a rock. It looked ordinary, just a smooth black river rock. But his grandfather did nothing without a purpose, so he slipped it back in, knowing the reason for it being there would reveal itself in time.

A few miles later, Pax felt a breeze blow through his hair, and he looked up. Ceya was following him. He smiled up at the red-tailed hawk who had watched over him for as long as he could remember. He wasn't alone, after all.

When he heard, "You never were," he smiled and nodded at the trees and lifted his eyes to the clouds, and placed his hand on his heart. Whatever happened, he would do his best. He hoped it would be enough.

NINE

The High Priestess known as Isira lowered her head and smiled at the young man standing in front of her. Akotas had told her to call Pax when it was time to prepare him for his journey, and he had answered her call.

Isira wasn't sure she was the right person for the job, but Akotas had assured her that Pax was sturdier than he looked and would listen to her instruction. Isira tried to tell Akotas that the boy wasn't the problem. She was.

"One failure doesn't make you a failure," Akotas said.

"Perhaps not. But it doesn't bode well for success either."

They argued for days and finally came up with a solution. Akotas would do his part with Pax, leaving only the last part of the training to her. And because Isira still wasn't sure it was enough, Akotas agreed to do one more thing. He would provide Pax with a guardian for his journey.

Isira yielded, and Akotas returned to the forest to tell Pax of his destiny. It wouldn't be the entire truth, but it would be close enough that Pax would have to develop enough courage to step into his future. No, Pax was not a warrior. But he could change a mistake made before his time. One he and Isira had let happen. Not let happen—didn't stop from happening.

Isira smiled at Pax. He was a beautiful young man. That wasn't surprising, considering his lineage. Now that Pax stood before her, Isira understood why Akotas had believed that Pax could fix what they had broken.

However, the light that shown out of him needed to be hidden. Where he was going, people didn't shine like that.

Now Isira understood what Akotas wanted her to teach Pax. He needed to learn how to look and act ordinary. She had taught others, including herself. The hardest part was not learning how to hide the light, but remembering how to bring it back. That had been one part of her failure. Perhaps she could stop that from happening to Pax.

She and Akotas had agreed she would be the one to tell Pax that Akotas was not his actual grandfather. She shook her head and wished that the past had never happened. But it had. And it was up to Pax to fix it.

• • • ● • ● • ● • •

Every day, Pax wished he could go back to his tree and hide. Isira's training was so much more challenging than Akotas' had been.

In the woods, he had learned about the trees and the community of nature, and how to be one with it. Isira tried to teach him how to be part of the community of the village. Pax found people much harder to understand than the animals and plants of the woods.

He hated the way they stared, looked away, and whispered to each other. Isira said it was because he was a stranger, and they were curious, but that made little sense to him. No animal ever pointed at him and then laughed behind his back. It didn't help that he looked nothing like the people in the village.

Their skin and hair were dark, their eyes deep brown like the bark on a tree. His skin was dark too, but only where the sun touched it. His hair was almost white. But it was his eyes that people stared at the most. He didn't know that his eyes were pale blue like a light-filled sky until Akotas told him, and he didn't realize that it mattered until he came to the village.

One night by the fire, he asked Isira to tell him the truth.

"What truth is that, Pax?"

"Am I grandfather's grandson?"

Isira paused and looked away. When she answered, Pax rose, ready to go back to the woods and never return.

"No. Not that way."

"In what way, then?"

"You are a descendant of the man who climbed the cliff. Each generation after him looked like our people, like the people of the woman he married. When you were born, your parents were afraid, not understanding why their child looked so different.

"They brought you to me and Akotas and asked for help. We agreed to because we believed we knew why you looked like the original peacemaker. Not long after that, the Satoka raided the village, and your parents died fighting to save many of our people and your life. They managed to get you to Akotas, and he kept you in the woods with him.

"That's why people point at you. You came from the woods. Akotas trained you. And yes, you don't look like them, and so they stare. But more than that, they wonder how you could be another peacemaker. If the Sakota attack again, you don't appear to be a warrior or a leader like Akotas was so how can you help them?

"Where is Pax's power, they ask themselves? Does Pax have any magic at all?

"And the more you retreat from them, the more worried they are. The only reason the people have some belief that you will help them is they see the light in you."

After absorbing and accepting what Isira told him, Pax made progress. He practiced listening to the people the same way he listened to the trees, plants, and animals of the woods. He stopped thinking about how strange they were and tried to understand what made them happy. He stopped caring how they felt about him.

Pax saved the village more than once when he felt the presence of the remaining Satoka and warned the village of the danger. In time, the people accepted him and believed that he might truly be the descendant of William Sky.

When Isira saw Pax comfortable among the people, she told him that soon he would leave to go to another world, where he would find people who didn't live as they did, and he would need to adjust to them quickly. His listening skills would serve him well.

She told him that while he was in the other world, Pax would meet Akotas' wife and child. He would rescue them and bring them back to Crann, and defeat Dradon.

Pax stared at Isira and started laughing. "Defeat Dradon? Seriously?"

When Isira didn't respond to his laughing, he did what Akotas had done years before. He got up and walked away.

Two weeks later, he returned.

"Tell me what I need to do," he said.

TEN

Stepping off the cliff was the scariest thing Pax ever did. But Isira had told him repeatedly he would not hit the ground. He would be in another world. Yes, she had been there. Do what she and Akotas had taught him to do. Listen. Yes, Ceya would come with him. She was looking forward to it.

But still. The idea of falling into space terrified Pax. Yes, he lived in a tree in the clouds. But this was going down, not up. However, he had made his choice. He needed to put away what he wanted, which was to return to the woods. He had to do what everyone told him was his purpose in life.

That he couldn't see what others saw didn't matter. There was no point in arguing. It was best to agree to what everyone wanted. That he was afraid—no, terrified—didn't matter. Besides, he was sure Isira knew he was afraid. After all, it would be hard to miss his trembling hand as Ceya perched on his arm. Ceya didn't seem afraid at all, so Pax tried to take courage from that.

Once he arrived in the other world and oriented himself, he would go to the address Isira gave him. Isira assured him he would understand the idea of addresses once he arrived. The land would look vaguely familiar. It was hard to hide three rivers. The difference would be buildings and roads and very few trees.

"So it's not another place?" Pax asked, still confused.

"No, same place. Another world. We've gone over this before, Pax. There are many other worlds, but this cliff only takes you to one. And yes, it has the same sun, the same stars, and yes, it is within the same time in the universe as this one. But there are many, many more people. It's crowded, Pax."

Pax looked across the vastness of the world they lived in, one where the villages nestled in the land's natural habitat, and couldn't imagine not living like that. If Dradon hadn't started fighting to become the one and only ruler of every village and every clan, they would have known nothing but peaceful cooperation. After Dradon left, the few remaining Satoka's rarely raided, and the peace Crann had always known was once more present.

"Not always, Pax," Isira said, reading his thoughts. "You know, it was your ancestor who brought peace to this world. Before then, there were more men like Dradon."

Pax had heard the story many times—how William Sky climbed the cliff and changed everything. That he was the descendant of that man gave him courage. But he wasn't climbing a cliff. He was falling off one. On purpose.

Once he arrived in the other world, he understood what his two jobs would be. Neither of which seemed possible, especially for someone like him. He was still processing that Isira and Akotas once lived in that world. Isira and Akotas had returned. Dradon had not. Isira said it was because Dradon liked the other world. More people to control. More power to gather. She could not make Dradon return. Pax would be the one to fix her mistake.

She and Akotas returned to take care of their people, although Akotas had not wanted to come back either. He had fallen in love. But Akotas had known his duty then, as Pax recognized his duty now.

When Pax learned that the man he called grandfather had a wife in another world, it answered something that Pax often wondered. In the past, when he asked Akotas about his wife, Akotas would always direct the question away.

Now he understood why. He wasn't Akotas' grandson, and Akotas' wife lived in another world.

"Why didn't he bring her back with him?" Pax asked.

"He did. Maya lived with us until their daughter was born, but Maya missed her world, and so they separated."

One last time, standing on the edge of the cliff, Pax asked again, "Why not leave them all alone? Since Dradon left, we have lived in peace."

Isira turned to look at Pax, her dark brown eyes glittering with tears. Pax felt her hands tremble on his shoulders, and he didn't know if that made him feel more loved or more afraid.

"Dradon has brought his evil ways to their world, which already had men like Dradon. We can't leave him there. It's only making it worse. It would be wrong for us to ignore what he is doing. He's from our world, after all. And we need someone to rule after I am gone. That would be Akotas' daughter."

Pax lowered his head to hide his tears, and without meaning to say it out loud, whimpered, "Why me?"

Isira pulled him close and whispered, "It's not just for these two worlds, Pax. It's for you, too. Trust me."

Pax raised his head and nodded and asked again, "How will I know Akotas' wife and daughter?"

Isira smiled then, put her hand on his arm, and looked him in the eye. She was almost as tall as him, which wasn't saying much since his short stature was another reason the villagers had first stared at him. Weren't warriors supposed to be tall and strong?

"But Pax isn't a warrior," Isira reminded them. "He has another role in life." But to Pax, she said he was a warrior, just a different kind of one. One that would require just as much courage, but much more than that. He would need the wisdom he learned in the woods from Akotas and in the village from her.

"There will be no doubt in your mind who they are. Besides, Ceya knows them."

Isira held up her hand as he started to ask how Ceya knew them, and Pax understood it was for Ceya to tell him.

"When you find them, take them to the address I gave you. There will be people there who can help you. People that know of more than one world and one time."

"What if they don't want to go?"

"Convince them," she said. "The mother will be the easiest. Once you have done that, the daughter will follow."

"And Dradon?"

"Once you have Maya and Ginny, Dradon will follow them because they have the power he wants. Let the people at that address help you. But it is up to you to make sure he returns so we can stop him."

Isira almost added, "Or you will have to destroy him," but she didn't. She trusted Pax to know what to do when the time came.

Smiling at Pax with tears still in her eyes, she added, "Your gift of listening will serve you well, but use your other gifts too when necessary."

Pax nodded. What else could he do? He heard Isira's heart breaking, her worried thoughts that she hadn't done enough for him, her fear he would fail.

He understood it embarrassed Isira that Pax saw her weakness. But she was also proud of him. And that was what he was going to hold on to, to get him through what came next.

Isira reached out and hugged him again as hard as she could, and when he turned back to the cliff, she gave him the slightest nudge, for which he was grateful. The nudge tilted him off the cliff and took away the moment of indecision. There was nothing left to do but fall and trust.

ELEVEN

Valerie Price looked out her front window and sighed with happiness. She loved living in the very center of the village of Doveland. Across the street, a beam of sunlight glanced off the roof of the gazebo. The dew on the grass sparkled, and daffodils and tulips filled the flower beds. Valerie thought everything about the park was perfect. It was both beautiful and functional.

The street that went around the park branched off in four directions like arrows of the compass. Everyone coming or leaving town eventually passed by her house.

She realized some people might not enjoy having so much activity going by their house, but Valerie did. For her, it was like living within the heart of the town, filled with people she loved. Valerie recognized almost everyone who lived in Doveland. For years she had been the high school principal. And she had run the town council until last fall when she decided it was time for someone else to be in charge.

The front windows of her home were the perfect lookout for friends and even for the rare stranger that passed through. Doveland was far away from any main road which kept it a quiet place to live. Strangers didn't usually just pass through Doveland. They came for a reason.

But it wasn't just cars that circled the park. The traffic included bikes and runners and parents with strollers. Recently the town had added to the bike and walking paths that ran from the center of town west towards the village of Concourse. And now, both the walking and bike paths were being extended in the other three directions.

Valerie knew her friends were the ones extending the paths. Ava and her husband, Evan, supplied the funds, and Ava's uncle Hank provided the labor, assisted by the group of youngsters he and others in the village mentored. Her sons, Johnny and Lex, were recipients of the mentoring group, a fact for which she would remain forever grateful.

That was one reason checking out the town outside her window brought her so much pleasure. She watched over them as they watched over her. Valerie sighed again with happiness when she heard her husband Craig coming down the stairs. He had been out late delivering yet another child, but that wouldn't stop him from being at the town's clinic all day as Doveland's doctor. Craig remained one of the main reasons for her continued happiness. He was part of the group of friends who had come to Doveland a few years before and changed the village and her life forever.

Valerie leaned back into Craig's arms, and he rested his chin on the top of her head as they observed the town come awake. Their youngest son, Lex, was in the kitchen making them breakfast before heading off to school. He loved to cook. He practiced by either cooking for them or helping Pete and his wife Barbara at the Diner that stood on the north side of the roundabout.

On the other side of the street from the Diner lay the coffee shop, Your Second Home. The Diner and coffee shop were favorite meeting places for everyone in town.

Craig and Valerie waved at the owner of the coffee shop as she stepped onto the sidewalk to water the pot of pansies that stood by the front door. Grace Strong waved back, pointed inside, and Valerie nodded. Both of them understood that meant Grace wanted to talk when Valerie had time. If it were urgent, Grace would have texted, but the pointing meant, "come over when you can."

Lex called from the kitchen to come to breakfast. He had made blueberry pancakes and was already tucking into his stack by the time they reached the booth in the kitchen. Valerie smiled at her son and thanked him for breakfast. With a mouth full of pancakes, Lex gave his mother the thumbs-up sign.

Their house used to be a bed-and-breakfast, but after Valerie's first husband died, she and her friend Mindy had renovated the house and turned the back half of the lower floor into a design studio. However, when Mindy moved away with her husband, Tom, Valerie had moved the studio online. Instead of redesigning houses, Mindy's strength, Valerie now sold things the townspeople made to buyers worldwide. Her other son Johnny built and ran the site while finishing up his schooling at Penn State.

Yes, Valerie thought, *I am well taken care of.*

However, as Valerie listened to Lex talk about school, she realized something kept niggling at her. She wasn't sure if it was fear or anticipation. Because even though Grace had seemed casual about their meeting, she thought it was something more.

Not enough that it was urgent. Yet. But given their history, most likely someone was coming to Doveland who would need their help. The question always was, what kind of help, and how dangerous was it?

"Something on your mind, Valerie?" Craig asked.

"Hum. Not sure."

Without thinking about it, they both turned to look at Lex.

"Nope. Don't have a clue," he said, tucking back into the last few bites on his plate. Then kissing his mom on the head and high-fiving Craig, he grabbed his backpack and flew out the door, just in time to catch the school bus as it came around the circle.

"That should make me feel better," Valerie said, "Except he realized why we looked at him. Maybe he knows more than he's saying."

"Still," Craig said. "He didn't seem afraid. So if something or someone is coming, it might not be a bad thing."

"I suppose," Valerie said.

Craig looked over at his wife, her short brown hair curling around her face, and marveled at the forces that brought them together. They had passed through some terrifying times together, but he wouldn't trade it for anything.

"Val, it's been quiet for a few months. Perhaps you are hoping for some kind of mystery to solve."

"I suppose," Valerie said again, standing up to hug him. She would never tire of his arms around her or stop being proud of his commitment to being the best possible doctor, one dedicated to the prevention of problems, which meant he spent much of his time doing things for free.

"Go see Grace," Craig said, giving her a tiny push. "I'll wash up."

Valerie laughed, grabbed her purse and phone, kissed Craig on the cheek, and ran out the door.

Craig watched her run across the street towards the coffee shop and then ran his hand through his hair. Yes, he felt it too. Someone was coming for help, and as always, there was someone else who wanted to stop them. But it felt different this time. Who knew if that was good or bad. Usually, it was both.

Craig sighed and turned to clean up the kitchen. There were people he knew who needed him now, and that's where his attention had to be. If Valerie and Grace needed him, they knew where to find him.

TWELVE

I t took Pax a minute to realize that he hadn't shattered into a million pieces at the bottom of the cliff. Instead, he stood within a ring of trees that looked like the trees from his world. Except his trees grew much larger. These trees barely reached into the sky.

But at least they are trees, Pax thought.

Not many of them. It wasn't a forest that extended for miles, and that seemed so strange to Pax that he had to stare for a while to make sense of it. From where he stood, Pax could see outside the stand of trees to what he would have called a meadow. Except it was mostly green, and all the green was the same height.

Why would that be? Pax asked himself.

What hit Pax next was the noise. He held his hand over his ears, trying to figure out what it was and where the sounds came from.

"Nowhere and everywhere," he heard Ceya say. But not in his head. It was a human voice that spoke out loud.

He turned in circles, looking up into the trees, looking for the hawk, but he didn't see her.

"Not there, here," Ceya said, stepping out from behind the trees.

Pax stepped back, tripped over a tree root, and fell, still staring at the young woman standing in front of him.

"Shut your mouth, Pax. And get up."

"But you are a bird, not a woman."

Ceya laughed, and Pax heard the hawk's call within the laughter.

"I can't be a talking bird in this world. I would be trapped and trained. That is, if I was lucky. It's too dangerous for me to be a bird here. So I'm a woman. How do I look?"

Pax had used a tree to help himself off the ground, and now he kept his hand on its trunk, needing whatever energy and understanding the tree would give him. At first, he felt it resist, and then it sighed beneath his fingers and sent soft, soothing waves of energy to him.

He returned waves of gratitude to the tree and then turned to Ceya.

"You're beautiful, Ceya."

He spoke the truth. Ceya's soft white fluffy hair curled about her face. She wore a dress that ruffled in the wind. Although her eyes were a dark gray, when the sunlight glinted off them, he saw a hint of her red hawk eyes.

"You look good too, Pax, but we need to do something about your clothes. If you can make yourself invisible while we find some, that would be a good idea."

Pax disliked being invisible. He couldn't hold it for long, was never sure when it would fade and reveal him, and it always drained him of energy.

"What's wrong with these?"

"Well, you appear to be something out of an old west movie," Ceya answered.

Isira had filled him in with some details of the world he would find himself in, so he knew what a movie was and even had a vague idea about what kind of movie Ceya meant. But still.

"So, what?"

Ceya turned to Pax. She, like Isira, was as tall as him. Pax hoped people didn't tease him for being small in this world, but figured that was the least of his worries.

"It is the least of your worries," Ceya affirmed, reading his mind as she had done as his protector all these years. "And if you don't mind people staring at you as if you are from another world, okay. But I would think we would want to fit in a bit more. However, if you insist, we'll leave you as you are."

Ceya turned and starting walking so quickly that Pax had a moment of wondering if her feet were actually touching the ground. Catching up, he asked where they were going.

"You mean now or later?"

"Ceya, cut it out. You know I mean now. Don't we have to find Akotas' wife and daughter?"

"We do. But they won't be hard to find. Especially since Koda has been watching over the wife."

"Koda?"

Ceya didn't stop. If anything, she moved faster, rushing through the green prickly stuff he now realized was called grass, and yelled back at him, the wind barely carrying her words: "My husband."

• • • ● • ● • • •

"Husband? You have a husband?" Pax yelled at Ceya since she was now yards ahead of him and moving faster. Even if she had wanted to, she probably couldn't have heard him. The noise kept getting louder. It was so horrible he couldn't think. At least now he could see what Isira had told him were cars and trucks in the distance, and he knew they were making much of the noise.

Concluding that he had made a horrible mistake made him want to find the cliff, climb it, and return to his world. The quiet one. The one where he lived alone, high in the tree of life, wrapped in a cloud. Here the trees were too small, and the clouds too far away.

But Pax reminded himself that Akotas had protected and taught him his entire life. He owed it to Akotas to stay and find Akotas' wife and his daughter. Pax kept conveniently forgetting that he was also supposed to find and stop Dradon.

But at that moment, he needed to find Ceya. Without her, he was well and truly lost.

"Look up, fool," he heard in his head.

Peering up into the sky that was almost as blue as the sky of his world, he observed two hawks circling around and around, riding the wind.

"Walk a little more, and you'll discover a building. Go inside and wait for us. We'll be there in a little while."

Pax pushed back, "Take your time, Ceya," not just for her and the joy that radiated from her, but for him. It would give him time to figure out what to do next, and he felt extraordinarily tired. *Perhaps because of the fall, and the noise, and this horrible green prickly stuff*, Pax reflected, walking as quickly as possible across it, heading for another stand of trees where he glimpsed a small gray building. He sighed, grateful for having found it. He needed to sleep.

Slipping in the open door, he stepped into a small room. A quiet room. It's almost like a nest, Pax realized as he curled up on the floor, covering himself with a blanket that had been hanging off a chair. Within minutes he was asleep, dreaming of his world, while two hawks circled and dived above him.

THIRTEEN

Something had happened. He'd been standing in front of the six men he called his board of directors to their faces—but even they knew they were only sycophants—when a massive wave of pain slammed through his head.

It took all Dradon's self-discipline not to scream. He turned away, hoping no one would see his hands shaking, and pretended to be looking at the papers he'd brought with him and put on the chair behind him. Dradon never sat. He always stood, looking down at the people staring at him. He loved that they thought of him as a god. Why not? He ruled their lives.

As they waited, no one gave away that they were impatient or upset. Even if he didn't speak for an hour, they would sit, eyes cast down, pretending everything was okay, afraid to move or speak even to ask if something was wrong.

Especially that. Never ask Dradon if something was wrong—nothing could ever be wrong.

"If there's a problem, don't tell me about it, because I can read the problem inside of you. I don't need to hear it again. Just tell me what you are doing to fix it," he would hiss.

Dradon's first board of directors didn't believe him and rebelled against his way of doing things. They didn't last long—except for one. One who remade himself in his boss's image. He did what Dradon wanted, never questioned orders. He always came up with imaginative ways to deal with anything that didn't work out how Dradon wanted it to be.

Fred Smith's effectiveness was a double-edged sword to Dradon. Fred excelled at his job, followed orders, and kept quiet. But Dradon sometimes wondered if Fred was playing with him. However, he couldn't eliminate Fred based on suspicion, or because he hated Fred's ordinary name, or his passive way of standing and speaking, could he?

So Fred sat with the other six men, heads hanging, waiting for him to speak.

But all he said was, "Get out!"

Without a sound, the seven men gathered their papers and slipped out the door, closing it softly behind them. Dradon followed them with his eyes and then listened as they walked away. They knew enough not to speak. But he checked on them, anyway. He didn't want a whisper of anything that suggested weakness to be spread about him.

He learned long ago how to send a pulse of pain to someone when they displeased him. He trained them like the animals because that's how he thought of them. Animals that did his bidding. Which meant they stayed silent as they headed to their separate offices.

Once he was alone, Dradon collapsed onto the chair, not even bothering to remove the papers. He understood what the pain in his head meant. Someone had fallen from the cliff. Someone was coming after him.

Dradon clenched his teeth. He would never give up this world. This world was much more fun to manipulate than his world. Manipulating his world had been too easy. He formed the Satoka clan just to make trouble for his brother and sister. And parents. Well, all of them. Life had been too quiet. Boring actually. He persuaded a few people that the Decana were greedy and unfair. He told people lies, and they believed him. That's when he learned that there were always people who wanted to fight, and they would believe anyone who told them anything that gave them an excuse to do so. He created division.

William Sky had climbed the cliff to heal divisions and bring peace and he, Dradon, had torn that peace apart with a few words. Yes, it had been too easy.

So when he and Akotas fell off the cliff, the fall turned out to be the best thing that ever happened to him. He found a world that was already divided. A world that was already following people who wanted to fight. Becoming the most powerful man among those men would be a challenge, and he wanted in on it.

He and Akotas had separated as they fell. Akotas landed close to the cliff and the three rivers, but he landed in the middle of a city. Luckily for him, although he didn't believe in luck, he had arrived in a park where he hid as he figured out the world and who he wanted to be.

It didn't take him long to adjust. He found plenty of people to steal from. Whatever he wanted, he took. He learned he needed two names, not like in Crann, where one was enough. So he called himself Dradon Good. He found that funny since he was the opposite of good, and everyone knew it. He even liked it when some people called him The Dragon once he learned what dragons were. Yes, he obliterated landscapes. Sometimes literally. If he wanted something, he took it. He divided. He ruled.

The last time someone fell off the cliff it had been Isira coming to take him and Akotas home. She failed with him. Perhaps she sent someone else. Not Akotas. Akotas accepted what he had told him. That his wife and daughter would be free to live peacefully as long as he didn't interfere with Dradon's work in this world.

It was too bad Akotas trusted him. Yes, he had left Maya and her daughter Ginny alone. In a way. He kept Maya living in constant fear he would hurt her daughter, but since he could have easily eliminated them both, in his own way he kept his promise to Akotas.

Dradon didn't think it was Isira, either. She would be ruling and would not leave that obligation. It was her loyalty to that obligation that forced her to leave him in this world so many years before.

Actually, she failed with them both. Akotas met Maya and didn't want to return, although he did later. And he, well, he discovered a world where he could stretch out his abilities and control people and events as if they were his playthings.

So who had come for him? He had killed the descendants of William Sky. There was no one left with any power.

Dradon stood, feeling better. It must have been something other than what he assumed it was. Still, perhaps it would be best to send Fred to watch over Maya. He would keep his promise to Akotas, but only if no one was coming after him.

If they were, Fred Smith, the man with the ordinary name who looked like someone could blow him over by breathing on him, would know what to do.

FOURTEEN

After waving at Valerie and then pointing to her shop, Grace Strong stood outside for a minute, watching the light creep into the park. Like Valerie, Grace loved the park with its benches, flower beds, and trees. The redbud and the apple trees grew at the south end of the park. And now that they were blooming, she could barely see the grocery store that sat opposite her store on the roundabout.

A new pine tree now stood in the center of the park. The town decided it would be wonderful to decorate a live tree each year rather than cutting one down. She thought that was a wise decision. She smiled to herself. Another reason she loved where she lived now. Although she had lived in many places and always found a reason to love where she lived, this was the first place that felt like home.

Inside her coffee shop, Grace made sure everything was exactly how it should be before her first customers of the day arrived. She loved coming down in the morning and preparing the space. She had hired baristas, so she was no longer needed behind the counter unless she wanted to be, and a pastry chef made sure there were always fresh pastries available. Sometimes she made her famous scones, and once in a while, Alex or Pete brought their cooking classes over, and they made pastries for her.

As she often did, Grace stood in the center of her store and smiled. This place was a dream come true. She had always wanted to provide a space where people felt welcome and safe, and now it existed for real, and not just in her imagination. Actually, it was better than she had ever imagined.

Although she was constantly tweaking things to make them better, it didn't stop her from thinking that it was perfect right now. The rich, warm scent of fresh coffee and pastries seeped into every corner of the spacious room. There were bookshelves filled with books to read and buy if you wanted to take one home. Small tables were available where people held private conversations, or read, or worked on their computers. And there were large tables to gather with a group. She designed the room in such a way sound didn't travel, making it either a quiet or lively space depending on what you needed on any given day.

It was also where Grace kept tabs on everyone in Doveland. Like Valerie, she loved knowing what was going on with everyone in town. When she was young, Grace disliked being short and plump. Now, older and wiser, she loved it. With her short dark gray hair, glasses around her neck, and deep brown eyes, she looked like everyone's picture of the warm-hearted grandmother. Everyone told her things, or she figured them out by watching and listening.

Being the town's busy body became a label she wore with pride because she knew her heart's intent was to be helpful. And she was. She had been that way as long as she could remember, but now it was out in the open. Everyone knew if you needed help, ask Grace. If she can't help, she will find someone who can.

The first people Grace would go to for extra help were her council of women, all of them deeply connected friends. The council of women met every Monday night in her apartment above the store. They always had good things going on. Only they, and the ones closest to them and who helped them, were aware of all they did, and that's the way they wanted it.

Most of what the women (and the men in their lives) did remained ordinary, like providing families with food or taking care of someone's rent or mortgage. They did it all quietly and effectively. However, there were always the other things, things people might not believe could happen or exist, that they helped resolve.

It seemed to Grace that Doveland attracted quite a few people who needed the unique help they offered. Perhaps some kind of cosmic bulletin board existed that listed them as a resource.

Although Grace could not do many of the things some of her friends did, over the years her sense of awareness had increased, and now that she hung around with people who did what others considered "magical," it seemed that had rubbed off on her.

Perhaps when you see things most people consider impossible and realize they are not only possible but common, it opens other doors of perception. That's what Grace figured had happened to her. Instead of being a small-town busybody, she was a cosmic busybody. She accepted it as a good thing because otherwise, she might resent that she was often awakened at night, and sometimes interrupted in her day, with a sense of something coming.

Instead, she thought of it all as an adventure. And now, she was sure another adventure was coming to Doveland, which is why she signaled for Valerie to come over. She wanted to find out if Valerie had felt it, or perhaps Lex had told her something. Lex's burgeoning ability to remote-view had helped them prepare last time. Maybe he was aware of something now.

Grace left the door unlocked, as she did every morning once she came downstairs. All the locals appreciated that even when she wasn't officially open if she was downstairs and someone needed their morning quiet, coffee, or a scone, they were welcome to come in. She called her store Your Second Home because that was what she wanted it to feel like. A safe space where everyone was always welcome.

While she waited for Valerie, Grace poured herself a cup of coffee and, with only a moment's hesitation, grabbed a cranberry scone and settled into a booth where she could both relax and watch the front door. If she was right about the dreams she was having, it wouldn't be long before someone walked through the door who she didn't know. She needed to be ready.

FIFTEEN

F red ordered his coffee and then headed back to his car as he observed a group of children walk by. Four women walked with them, and he knew one of them was his target. He glanced at his phone and Ginny's picture and smiled to himself.

Yes, there she was, looking just as Dradon described. He had his orders, and he intended to follow them to the letter, in his way. Dradon was right. She was beautiful. She had a delicate beauty that took a few minutes to notice. Fred snickered to himself. He would have many minutes to notice, and he planned to take advantage of all of them.

Fred had a gift. He understood how to bend to people and circumstances and how to blend into his surroundings. He easily became a nobody, even to Dradon, who should know better than to trust what appeared on the surface. However, Dradon realized Fred was capable and believed he followed orders. After all, Dradon sent him to observe and then eliminate, if necessary, more than once. And he always did both, with no one realizing he had been there.

What Dradon hadn't noticed about Fred was his ability to deceive. Dradon didn't notice because he didn't care. As long as no one associated him with what Fred did, Dradon remained happy. Fred was happy, too. His assignments always gave him time to practice his skills and satisfy his need to control everything. Not that he let anyone see that need in him. Instead, they saw a capable servant. All part of the plan. Someday he would take over from Dradon. It was a time-honored tradition. The follower overthrows the master. But not now. Only when the time was right. And when that time came, Fred would make sure there would be no doubt in anyone's mind of his ability to be the man in charge.

It pleased Fred no one would ever suspect him of having a desire or intent to be the head of Dradon Good's empire. He presented himself as the perfect lackey. No one would believe that this average-looking, too skinny, too small, balding, glasses-wearing man with his meek exterior was capable of anything other than being a quiet, compliant servant of the great Dradon Good.

Fred thanked whatever gods had given him this nerdy appearance. Once he realized the power his appearance gave him, he used what he looked like to his advantage. He cultivated a way to disappear. It eliminated fighting. It eliminated competition. In his enemies' eyes, Fred wasn't dangerous. They didn't even know they were his enemies. He was an unseen, unknown disease, and he was eating away, slowly but surely, Dradon Good's empire.

He believed that this girl Ginny might be the key to destroying it forever. So yes, it delighted him when Dradon sent him on this simple mission.

"Monitor her," he said.

"That will be a pleasure," Fred answered, Dradon not understanding how much of a pleasure it would be for Fred.

Stepping out of his car, Fred put the first part of his plan into action. Meet Ginny. No, it wasn't what Dradon asked. But what did that matter? Meeting her would make it easy to watch over her, and in the end, that's what Dradon wanted. And that's what he would give him.

That it would also enable him to discover what made Ginny and her mother important to Dradon made it even more pleasurable. And it certainly didn't hurt that Ginny was beautiful. He planned to enjoy the time he spent with her to the fullest.

· · · ● · ● · ● · ·

One thing Ginny learned from her mother was to observe everything. Perhaps there were other things her mother taught her that had faded into the background, but recognizing what was happening, what was different, and how it felt, had been drilled into her as long as she could remember.

So as she crossed the street with the three mothers who had volunteered to go along with her on the school trip to the museum, she noticed the man with the glasses sitting in the car. She knew he was watching her and the children.

So when he stepped out of the car and came towards her, she saw him coming. For a moment, she felt uneasy, and then when he smiled at her, that feeling vanished, and she thought she had been mistaken. So Ginny smiled back and waited to find out what he needed.

SIXTEEN

"Excuse me," Fred said, "But I saw you and the children and wondered what school you are from. My daughter and I are moving here, and before I buy or rent a house, I wanted to check out the best place to live based on the schools."

Ginny signaled to the three women to get the children onto the bus before telling him the school's name and its location.

"Do you think it would be okay to visit?"

"I don't see why not. Call and make an appointment with the school secretary first, though," Ginny said as she started up the steps of the bus.

"Appreciate it. Would you mention that I will call? My name is Fred Smith. Easy to remember, right?"

Ginny nodded and then, thinking she was being rude, reached down and shook his hand, saying, "I'm Ginny Maguire. What grade is your daughter in?"

"First."

"Well, perhaps I will see her in my class."

Fred smiled as Ginny stepped up onto the bus and waved at the children as they drove away.

That was a good start, he thought. He'd see her soon. After all, he needed to check out what kind of classroom his fictional daughter would be attending.

Ginny glanced out the back window as the bus pulled away and noticed Fred standing on the curb with a coffee cup in his hand, looking like a lost puppy, waving goodbye to the children, and wondered why he only said that he had a daughter, never mentioning a wife. Perhaps he was a single man raising a daughter. She understood what it felt like to be missing a parent. If that were the case, she would keep an extra watchful eye on his daughter.

Ginny appreciated that the man was being careful about choosing his daughter's school, so the next day it didn't surprise her when she saw him in the hallways. After a brief chat, she invited him to come and watch the classroom.

"Are you sure it won't be a bother?"

"Absolutely not," she replied, thinking again what a sweet man he appeared to be.

After spending an hour observing the children, he said he loved what was going on but needed to get to work. However, he still had a few questions. Would Ginny have coffee with him after school?

For a long moment, Ginny stood thinking if this was the right thing to do. But then, it was only coffee, and he was so quiet and unassuming, what could it hurt? It had been a long time since she had allowed herself to have a conversation with someone new. Perhaps she could be helpful to him if she understood more about his daughter and what she was like.

After he left, Ginny's teacher's aide whispered, "He's kind of cute in a different kind of way. Is he married?"

Ginny shook her head and said, "It's only coffee, and I don't know."

Later, Ginny would recall that her first instinct was to be wary of the man who stepped out of the car, but at that moment, she was so lonely she was grateful for the distraction. Coffee after work would differ from going home to a house that looked as if it would fall over at any moment, and a mother who refused to speak.

SEVENTEEN

The two red-tailed hawks circling above the park were not doing anything extraordinary to an ordinary observer. They could not have known how magnificent a reunion was taking place in the sky.

But Maya was not an ordinary observer. There was a reason she came to this park every day. Yes, she needed a place to go, but she could pick many other places. Museums, gardens, other parks, rivers, even coffee houses, and sometimes—out of pure frustration at the life she lived—she visited those places.

But she always came back to this park. Having done so for years, she knew the trees and plants better than she knew her own house. No matter the weather, she had places she found shelter, even if it was in her car.

Yes, there was a reason she came back to this park. She was waiting, hoping, praying that what she saw so many years before would repeat itself. Akotas would return and take her back. She hoped and prayed, even though she understood he probably wouldn't.

But what else could she do? She couldn't give up hope. Hope kept her alive. Hope kept her believing it was possible, because without it she had nothing. If Akotas couldn't come for her, Maya hoped he would send someone else. Someone who would save her and Ginny from what she had done. She chose to come back to this world. It had been the wrong choice. She realized that now.

What did she think would happen? Did she really believe Akotas could leave his duties as a protector of his clan, the clan that protected all of his world, the world he called Crann?

Akotas stayed with her in her world for a short time, but she understood he was unhappy. Her world was too loud and had too many people. And the skills he had did not translate to anything necessary for a job.

In fact, the concept of getting a job was entirely foreign to Akotas. In his world, people did what they did to live, not to make money to live. They traded and worked together. Each person fulfilled a purpose they felt deep within themselves or were born to do, like Akotas and Isira. And Dradon.

Except Dradon was different. So different that, unlike Akotas, he fit perfectly in this world. By the time Isira found him, Dradon had discovered that this world suited him to a tee. He discovered he fit into the competitive world of commerce, and he stayed. This world would be his home. It was where he was supposed to be. Yes, he would rule. He knew how to rule. It had been bred in him for centuries. But the ruling he would do here was so much more fun than in Crann.

Here he could make people fight against each other to his benefit. Here there were others like him to learn from and then destroy when they became useless. The ways to eliminate were endless. This world would never bore him. Here there was a power and energy that fed him. This world made him better and gave him purpose.

So no, he wouldn't go back. So Isira left both Dradon and Akotas and returned alone. Dradon stayed for power, but Akotas remained for love. Then one day, Maya realized she kept Akotas from being himself by asking him to live in her world. She would never forget the look he gave her when she told him she, and the baby she carried, would go with him to Crann. It was a look Maya treasured, and when the flame of hope within her faded, she would take herself back to that day. He loved her. She loved him.

She nurtured the hope that someday he would feel her distress and rescue her. Yes, she should have stayed in Crann. Instead, she returned, and Dradon condemned her to this life. She didn't understand why. She and Ginny were not a danger to him, especially now that he was so powerful. Perhaps it was his hatred of his brother and sister. Or did she know something that he wanted to know? If so, she didn't know what it was.

What she understood was she would never be free without help. It was why she came to the park every day. Because even if Akotas and Isira had forgotten her, she knew they would not let their brother ruin this world. Eventually, someone would come, and she would be there, waiting.

But there was one more reason she came to this park. Koda. Although they never spoke, never even acknowledged each other except to wave, she knew who he was. And she knew that he, too, was waiting for someone.

And today was that day. Someone had come.

Maya didn't see her arrive, but looking up at the two hawks, she knew who they were. Ceya and Koda. And since these two hawks had been the guardians of Akotas' family for years, it meant Ceya brought someone with her.

So Maya's heart soared with them, celebrating and acknowledging their great love for each other. At the same time, she mourned because she knew it was not Akotas who arrived with Ceya. If it had been him, he would have found Maya, not caring that she looked so old and worn away. He wouldn't have noticed. Instead, he would have run to her, and they would dance in the woods together, as Koda and Ceya were dancing in the sky.

No, it hadn't been Akotas who arrived. Maya tried not to let sadness overcome her joy. After all, she couldn't expect him to leave his world again for her. But perhaps Ceya and whoever came with her, were sent by him, and she would see him again soon. The day she stepped off the cliff, clutching Ginny in her arms, Akotas promised her he would see her again someday.

That promise kept her going all these years. She would not let go of that hope now.

EIGHTEEN

When Pax woke, he had a moment of complete disorientation. There was no sky above him, and the air smelled stale instead of sweet. Then he remembered the cliff, seeing Ceya as a woman instead of a hawk, and finally stumbling into this room.

He closed his eyes again, moaning to himself, and finally forced himself to sit up. Ceya sat on the floor in front of him, her eyes closed, head drooped, sleeping, just as she did when they slept in the tree. Except now, she was a woman and not a hawk, and they were no longer in Crann or in a tree.

Pax stifled the urge to lie back down, curl up, and return to sleep, where he would dream about his own world and his home in the trees and clouds. Instead, he reminded himself that he had a mission, and he couldn't return home until he did what he had come here to do.

Ceya opened one eye, then the other, and asked, "Feeling better, Pax? We brought food."

A man sat down beside Ceya, holding a plate of fruit and what looked like round bread. At least he recognized the fruit.

"Come on, eat, Pax. I expect you have questions, but it takes a lot of energy to move between worlds. You need food before starting out into this world. Besides, we need to teach you a few things, so you look as if you belong here."

Pax didn't bother arguing. He was hungry and confused, and despite his sleeping, he still felt exhausted.

"Why aren't you tired, Ceya?" he asked, once he had eaten enough to satisfy his gnawing hunger pains. The round bread with a hole in the middle was surprisingly good and filling.

Koda and Ceya turned to look at each other, and because he knew they were both hawks, he observed the slight tilt of their heads and the flash of red in both their eyes as they did so. Although Ceya had soft white curly hair and Koda's hair was red and quite straight, they looked alike, even in their human form. They fit together, the same way he had seen birds fit together as they sat on tree branches surveying the world.

"I've been here before, Pax. I'm used to this world. Well, not used to it. I mean, who could get used to it?" Ceya said, looking at Koda, her face so close to his their noses almost touched.

Very birdlike, Pax thought.

"I don't understand," Pax said. "When were you here?"

"It's rather a long story, Pax," Ceya said. "But the short version is this. As you know, Koda and I have been protectors of the leaders of the Decana clan for many of what this world calls centuries. So when Akotas and Dradon fell off the cliff, Koda instinctively went with them."

Ceya paused, and she and Koda exchanged looks before she added, "It was almost the worst moment of my life. I wanted to follow, but Isira had not fallen, and I had to stay. When she came to find them, I was more than delighted to come with her."

"And you found them?"

"We did, as you know. I realize you want all the details, but for now, all you need to know is it led to what actually became the worst moment of both our lives."

"What happened?"

This time Koda answered. "When Isira couldn't convince her brothers to return to Crann, we had to willingly part again, not knowing how long it would be—if ever—until we were together again. I stayed to watch over Akotas and Dradon. Ceya had to return with Isira."

Ceya sighed and laid her head on Koda's shoulder. Both of them closed their eyes, and Pax looked away, ashamed at himself for wishing he could go home.

"So if we accomplish our mission here, you both will return to Crann?"

"I don't know, Pax," Koda said, swiveling his head back towards Pax but holding Ceya close to him.

"If anyone from Crann stays here, I will have to remain, and Ceya will have to return to you and Isira."

"You mean Akotas' wife and daughter. What if they don't want to?"

"If that's what they decide, I will have to stay. But it's more than that, Pax. It's Dradon. As Isira told you, we can't let him remain in this world. Either he has to return to Crann, and be dealt with there—which is dangerous because he still has followers in Crann—or we have to eliminate him here."

"Eliminate? You mean kill him? No, I can't and won't do that. No."

"No?" Ceya said.

"No."

"Well, if you won't, we will. We are hunters, after all."

"But can't we find another way to stop him? Or force him to return to Crann?"

Ceya reached out and held Pax's hand between hers. For a minute, he thought he perceived claws, but the sensation quickly disappeared. Perhaps he felt claws because he knew her as a hawk and only imagined them.

"Yes, it's possible that there is another way. Perhaps something will happen that will help us. But it would be best if you prepared yourself for what we, and maybe you, need to do before any of us can go home. And you have to resign yourself to the idea that your mission is more important than how you personally feel."

Pax turned his head away, once more embarrassed about what he saw as his weak nature. It didn't matter that Akotas had told him he wasn't weak; he was different, and that difference was his strength. He had to believe that to be true if he wanted to help Akotas' wife and daughter and do what seemed impossible to him. Stop Dradon. Somehow.

Koda and Ceya stood as Ceya said, "Sleep more, Pax. You're safe here. When you wake, we'll begin."

Pax didn't need to be told again to sleep. He felt as if his whole body was pulling him into the earth, and he fell asleep the minute his head touched the ground.

Ceya covered him with the soft blanket Koda had hung on the chair, and turning to her husband, reached for his hand. If Pax were still awake, he would have heard them both giggling as they ran outside and flew. As they rode the air currents they could see everything laid below them: where three rivers became one, the streaming traffic, and even the woman who observed them.

As Maya saw the hawks circle above her, tears ran down her cheeks. She knew they had come for her. It was terrifying, knowing that Dradon would do anything to stop them and her, but it was also exhilarating because now there was a chance she and Ginny would be free. If not her, at least Ginny. She would make sure of that, no matter what it took.

NINETEEN

Instead of sitting in the coffee shop, Valerie and Grace took their coffees out to one of the park benches to watch the sunrise and listen to the dawn chorus. Tree frogs joined in the songs of the birds as a slight breeze whispered through the branches. Both of them understood that spring wouldn't last long. It was as if all of nature stored up energy through the winter and then, in a great burst, released it all at once. Spring was not a time to get distracted from the beauty of nature.

From where they sat, they could see masses of color. The delicate redbud with its rosy pink flowers looked beautiful alongside the white blooms of the cherry, apple, and magnolia. One of the many gardening groups in town had planted beds of tulips, hyacinths, and daffodils along the gravel paths. Later they would plant beds of flowers designed to attract bees, birds, and butterflies during the summer.

Grace sighed and laid her head back on the edge of the bench and watched the sky change from the dark blue of the night into the same color as a robin's egg.

"I love it here," she whispered.

Valerie smiled at her friend, thinking how grateful she was that Grace and her friends had chosen Doveland to make their home. She was sure that hadn't been their original intention, but once they arrived, they had changed Doveland—first by revealing a dark secret and then inspiring the changes that made Doveland such a beautiful place to live.

They also brought a different way of seeing and being that opened up possibilities for people to discover what some people called magic. Instead, it was what Valerie had come to understand was an expanded perception of what was possible.

Both her sons were benefactors of this expanded perception. At first, that scared her, but then she realized it was a gift. And like all gifts, they were only worth something if used.

"Did you ever hear that story about the sick whale?" Valerie asked.

Grace turned and smiled at her friend, shaking her head no.

"I wish I could remember all the details, but the story is that a whale had a disease that only one place in the world knew how to heal, and the whale swam there to get help."

"Smart whale," Grace said.

"That's what Doveland feels like to me. People come to us because we can help. And even though the whale brought with it a disease, the people at the hospital knew how to heal it."

"I can see how that applies to us," Grace responded. "Someone always seems to know how to help. Did Lex or Johnny mention anything about who is coming now?"

"Neither of them admit to having remote-viewed anyone. But you think there is?"

"Maybe it's only because of what you said about the whale. I know Doveland is the place people come to get help, so perhaps I am just expecting someone to show up since it's been a few months since our last adventure."

"Could be," Valerie answered. "But you expect it's more than that, don't you?"

"I do. And, it feels different this time."

Valerie laughed. "It's always different, my friend."

"That it is," Grace answered, and laid her head back on the bench.

"Might as well enjoy this quiet time while we have it," Valerie said, laying her head back on the bench like Grace.

And that's where Hank found them a few minutes later and asked them if they would like to have breakfast with him in the Diner.

"Why not?" they both replied, smiling at Hank as they stood and hooked their arms through his.

"Are you two up to something?" he asked.

"Not yet," they answered. And Hank, being Hank, understood what they meant.

• • • ● • ● • ● • • •

"Did you hear about the wind advisory for tomorrow?" Pete asked once Grace, Valerie, and Hank sat down.

"Spring wind," Grace said. "Perfect for scattering seeds."

"Well, that's one way to look at it," Pete said.

"I like wind most of the time, but it can be both good and bad, can't it?" Pete's wife, Barbara, said as she rounded the corner after coming downstairs from their apartment above the Diner.

"Like most things, I guess," she added. "I read that Paramahansa Yogananda said, 'Evil spreads with the wind; truth is capable of spreading even against it.'"

Grace and Valerie looked at each other before Grace said, "That kinda describes what Valerie was saying to me earlier."

"So evil is heading our way?" Hank asked.

"Along with someone who needs our help to fight it," Grace answered.

"Well, then I say eat up while we can," Pete said, laughing. "The usual for everyone?"

A round of nods of yes, and Pete headed to the kitchen to help Alex get their order ready. The morning crowd would arrive soon, and Alex would need all the help he could get. Alex Bender started as a server, then became a cook, and now he was not only the manager of the Diner, but he also helped with the cooking school he and Pete started for the children of Doveland and Concourse.

As Pete glanced around the Diner, he reflected on how much his life had changed from being a long-distance truck driver, which was how he and Hank had first met. These people had helped him and Barbara, so whoever was coming to Doveland to get their help, he was all in. Besides, it was another adventure, and Pete loved adventure. He wondered what kind was coming this time.

TWENTY

"It's time to learn your way around this world, Pax," Koda said the following day. "You've slept enough. Besides, Maya knows someone is here to help her, and I expect if we don't go talk to her soon, she will be at my door, demanding to know who else arrived from Crann."

Groaning as he sat up, Pax asked, "How would she know?"

"She saw Ceya and me flying. We made sure she would see us. Although we have never spoken, Maya knows I have been here and who I am. But because of Dradon, we have stayed away from each other. It was part of the agreement between her and Dradon. He would let Maya and Ginny live as long as no one ever learned about where he came from. But what Maya has been doing all these years is not living. It's surviving. And hiding. And hoping. Now you're her hope."

"I understand that is how you see me, but I don't understand how that can be. I came because I accept it is what Akotas and Isira want me to do. They told me it was me who has to help Maya and Ginny, but how? And stop Dradon? I understand what he is doing that I am supposed to stop, but don't know how I am supposed to do it. This world is not my world."

As Pax spoke, he became more and more agitated, walking around the parameter of the small shack, and each time around, his voice grew louder.

Koda watched, no expression on his face, his eyes tracking Pax's every move.

"Stop it!" Pax said. "When you look at me like that, I feel as if you are hunting me."

"Well, I am a hawk, after all," Koda smirked. "And in a way, I am hunting you. Hunting for the man who is supposed to help us all return to Crann. Where is that man? I only see a boy. Complaining and afraid."

"Well, we agree then. I am a boy, and I am afraid."

"What is wrong with you two?" Ceya demanded as she entered the shack, trying to hold the door with one hand and a bag in another.

The wind whistled through the open door, blowing papers across the floor and slamming the door against the wall.

Koda rushed to close the door as Pax took the bag from her hand and set it on the table.

"I thought I would introduce you to the pleasures of coffee in the morning, but I didn't count on that wind coming up. What are you two arguing about? If the wind weren't making so much noise, the entire neighborhood would have heard you. Including Maya, who is huddled out there in the car trying to stay warm."

"It's my fault," Pax said. "I'm complaining."

"And afraid I heard. Who could blame you? This is a strange world. But while we are here, and while Koda and I are in these bodies, there is no reason not to enjoy some of the pleasures it offers. Like this coffee and more bagels. Later we'll get you something else to eat, but first, try this."

Pax watched how Ceya and Koda opened their cup to drink and sigh with contentment. He did the same thing, took a drink, and spit it out.

"What is this stuff?"

"That was our first reaction, too," Ceya smiled. "But give it another chance. It will grow on you. And while we eat, let's plan our day."

· · · · ● · ● · ● · ● · · ·

Ginny's coffee with Fred went so well that they planned to meet again after school the next day at a park and have a small picnic. Ginny liked that idea. It kept their meeting casual, and it was good to have someone to talk to that wasn't her mother, who didn't speak to her, and children who were, well, children. And she had to admit it was a pleasure to talk to a man.

All her life, she'd been a loner. Ginny wasn't sure if that was who she was or because of who her mother had become. And she wasn't sure if she would ever find out. Life had handed her a script, and she couldn't rewrite it.

Living in what everyone called the haunted house hadn't helped. She couldn't invite friends over or even date unless she met them somewhere else. But once they found out what house she lived in, they stayed away from her. Sometimes they called her mother a ghost. Once she had a boyfriend, but it wasn't serious and didn't last long. Nothing could ever be serious. Even in college, she had stayed at home, too afraid to leave her mother by herself.

When Ginny was a young girl, she sometimes fantasized that she was a hero like Super Woman or even some actual women like Sally Ride who had courage and went after what they wanted. Fought for it. And lived life to the fullest. She would imagine the joy that would bring her to make things happen, to fight against evils in the world, stand up for what was right.

But Ginny stopped those daydreams when she accepted that none of that could happen because of her mother. And she loved her mother, despite what her mother was like now. She had memories of happier days. She remembered a beautiful woman holding her hand as they walked down the street, who bent over and kissed her every night, smelling like cupcakes.

So she stuffed down the urge to be someone and fight against injustice and instead taught, hoping she would do right by these children so they'd grow up and be who they were meant to be. She might not be able to do that for herself, but she could for them.

After their coffee yesterday, Ginny thought that perhaps she'd met someone who would understand her choices. She and Fred didn't talk about her mother. They spoke of him and his daughter. His wife died in childbirth, and he was raising her on his own. He traveled a lot in his job, which was why he was looking for an excellent school for his daughter. If she was happy in school, perhaps she wouldn't miss him as much.

Ginny asked Fred about his job, but he shrugged and said he was a quality control guy for a large firm. His job was to make sure everything flowed smoothly for his boss. Yes, he loved the work. But he was looking forward to a promotion, where he could stay in one place.

When he smiled at her, Ginny thought she would enjoy having him staying around. And then quickly dismissed the idea. She didn't want to put something into a relationship that wasn't even one. It was teacher and parent, that's it.

Still, having a picnic sounded good. Light and casual, just how Ginny wanted it. But neither of them counted on the wind that came up during the night.

So it didn't surprise Ginny when he texted and invited her to dinner instead. What she wasn't prepared for was how much she wanted to go.

TWENTY ONE

After making the phone call to Ginny to change their plans from a picnic to dinner, smiling to himself at how it was all working out, Fred did what Dradon asked him to do. Knowing that they were both at work, he went to Maya and Ginny's house to check it out.

Everything was a surprise to him. What Dradon hadn't told him was what the house looked like. Did Dradon know? It was falling apart. It reminded him of the house he had to walk by on the way to elementary school. Everyone called it the haunted house and stayed away. Even though he needed to walk by it to get to school, he would cross the street or take a long way around to avoid it if he were alone.

Sometimes he was with a group of kids who walked to school together, and then they would all point and shiver at the house, repeating all the ghost stories they had heard about it. They would push and shove, trying to make someone knock on the door. One day, Fred braved it. Tired of being the unwanted skinny boy in the group, he wanted to prove that he was worth something. He crossed the street, holding his breath, his hands balled into a fist, his backpack hanging heavy on his back, and walked up to the door and knocked.

The door was not opened by a ghost or a ghoul, but by a woman wearing an apron. She and the house smelled like cinnamon. He had stuttered and stammered, not having prepared anything to say. The only thing he had worked on was the courage to knock on the door. He, and the children hiding across the street watching him, had expected no one to answer.

The woman smiled, having glimpsed the children across the street, and realizing what was happening, invited him in. But not before making a growling sound and pretended to yank him inside. He stood, terrified until she returned with a plate of cookies. While he drank milk and ate cookies, she puttered around the kitchen. Once the cookies were gone, she sat down at the table with him. He remembered the table as if it had all happened yesterday.

The table had a shiny yellow surface, easy to keep clean, she said, and a silver metal edge. Many years later, he found a table like that in a junk shop, bought it, and restored it for his kitchen. That was before Dradon. Before, he had decided that men like Dradon, who thought they were gods, didn't deserve what they had.

He bought the table because it reminded him of the woman's kindness, a shining light in his life, changing everything. By inviting him in and then playing scary music and shrieking at him when he came out the door an hour later, it ensured him a place in his class as a brave boy, despite his weak-looking body and mild exterior.

So when Fred looked at Maya's house, he wasn't afraid. The woman he had met many years before let her house appear that way, so she would be left alone. Her husband had died. With no children to watch over her, she allowed the place to be her shield. Inside it had been warm and pleasant, and the hour he spent with her remained one of the happiest hours of his life.

Even though he hadn't known her, he had intended to do what she asked of him as she leaned over and kissed the top of his head and whispered, "Be a good boy, Fred."

But then life happened, and instead of being a good boy, he learned how to be a bad one. Still, there remained a soft spot in his heart that once in a while gave him trouble because he didn't want to be weak. Seen as weak was one thing. Being weak was an entirely different thing.

Fred parked around the corner and walked back to the house wearing a yellow vest that looked like what the town's maintenance crew wore and a hardhat on his head, carrying a clipboard. The neighborhood could be as nosey as they wanted to be, but they would only notice what he wanted them to see. A non-assuming maintenance guy, checking on a house.

The closer he got to the house, the more he smiled to himself, thinking that Ginny and her mother had done a great job of making it look like a haunted and neglected home. Bushes grew past the windows, the yard filled with weeds. Unattended rose bushes with thorns made it almost impossible to get up the tiny sidewalk to the door.

Although he knew no one was home, he knocked and stood patiently waiting, the clipboard hiding him as he unlocked the door. As he opened the door, he waved his hand in greeting, knowing that by doing so, nosey neighbors would assume someone asked him to come inside.

Fred stepped in and then turned behind the door, so it appeared as if someone else shut the door behind him. He shook his head as he looked at the interior of the home. He expected it to resemble the woman's home from his past. Warm and cozy inside, not at all falling apart, like the outside.

This house wasn't falling apart exactly, but it wasn't cozy and warm either. He glimpsed himself in the cracked mirror in the hallway and stared at the man he saw there. Yes, he looked exactly how he wanted to appear--unassuming, but confident and competent. He laid the clipboard down on the floor by the door, along with his hard hat, took out his phone, and started through the house.

Dradon ordered him to take pictures, so he did. It was an unwelcoming, impersonal space. Tidy, but not comfortable. He half expected to find an old yellow table in the kitchen, but the table that was there was only a beat-up wood table, looking as if it came from a junk pile or maybe was rescued from the side of the street before the trash men came.

Fred paused to take in the feeling of the house. Nothing. It felt like a shell or a facade. It was only in Ginny's room that he found a hint of life. A plant grew by the window. The walls were freshly painted a shade of blue, and her bed was covered with a multicolored quilt. Books were stacked on the side table, and a reading lamp hung over the bed. It was easy to see how Ginny spent her nights.

He took a picture of the books so he could brush up on what they were, something to talk about, but it wasn't something he would share with Dradon. The pictures he took of the room he would share made it look as sad as the rest of the house. He wasn't sure why he wouldn't give Dradon accurate pictures of Ginny's room, but he decided it was because it gave him information Dradon didn't know, and knowing what others didn't know was power.

A few minutes later, Fred walked out the front door, waved to the invisible person inside, and walked confidently back to his car after making a note on his clipboard, after glancing up at the roofline. Once again, a nosey neighbor might assume he had done an inspection of the house, and they might even believe that he would do something about its appearance. Obviously not. It would probably get worse once Maya and Ginny were gone. That was what Fred figured was Dradon's plan, and he would be the one who would take care of them. Why, he didn't know. But he intended to find out before doing so.

He needed to brush up on a few books before his dinner with Ginny. She had suggested the restaurant after asking him if he liked Indian food. He answered truthfully that he didn't know, but was looking forward to finding out.

TWENTY TWO

Maya spent the morning huddled in her car, which gave her very little protection against the cold. She knew how to make the car warm, just as she knew how to make the house look old. Akotas had taught her, but she resisted doing it.

It was only after she realized the wind would not stop blowing and she was achieving nothing by punishing herself by remaining cold that she relented and warmed up the car enough so she could think.

She was waiting to find out which of them would make the first move. She knew someone was inside the shack with Koda and Ceya and that Ceya had seen her in the car. Would they eventually come out and get her, or would she go in to them?

If she did, would she be putting their mission in danger? That was the last thing she wanted. She wanted Ginny to be saved. What that looked like, Maya didn't know. All she knew is that was what she wanted, and after all the time she had waited, she could wait a little longer.

Like I should get what I want, Maya muttered to herself. It was her fault they were in this mess. If she wasn't so adamant that she couldn't be herself in Crann, being afraid to conform to their way of life, they could have stayed there. What did she believe would happen when she returned to this world? That she could be herself? Not a chance. Dradon would never allow her that freedom.

Even though Maya understood that hate would not solve her problem, and as much as she was in the habit of berating herself, she hated Dradon. He deserved it. Maya believed if people learned who he really was, everyone would hate him. Well, everyone except those who were like him. There are plenty of them, she thought. Sometimes she wasn't sure if there were enough good people to make up for all the bad ones who only thought about themselves and power.

Yes, she had made the stupid choice to leave Crann because she wanted to be herself, in her world, and look at what happened. Now she didn't think about who she wanted to be anymore. After all, that was what got her in trouble in the first place. At least she tried not to think about herself, since she didn't deserve it. Sitting in the barely warm car, punishing herself for her past misdeeds, Maya allowed herself to remember when she first met Akotas.

That day, as she had done so many times before, she left the house to escape her parents' arguing and screaming at each other and had gone to her favorite spot in the park. Even though she knew it wasn't, she often imagined it as a secret space created especially for her. Sitting at the edge of the meadow, the trees at her back, watching birds fly above her, she saw a streak of light move from the sky to the ground. At first, she assumed lightning had struck, even though there was not a cloud in the sky.

When she saw a man rise in the meadow where the light had touched down, her first impulse was to run. But he was so beautiful, she couldn't. It was as if the light gave birth and produced this man. When he smiled at her, the world shifted on its axis. Later she asked herself if her parents arguing, her unhappiness, her sitting in the park at that precise moment had all been preordained.

He had walked over to her, sat next to her, and together they had gazed out on the meadow. Even though it had been only moments before that he fell out of the sky, Maya felt as if they had done this very thing for thousands of lifetimes. Later, once they got to know each other better, he told her it might be true. But on their first day, they simply let the light flow in and around them. Then he got up and walked into the woods.

Lying in bed that night, Maya decided she had dreamed the whole thing. Everything about it was impossible. But when she returned to the park the next day, he was waiting for her. And as if it were the most natural thing in the world, they sat together and talked.

When she asked him where he came from and where he lived, he smiled, took her hand, and said, "Nowhere." Then he asked her if she would teach him about her world. At first, she hadn't understood what he meant. She assumed he meant her life.

When she realized he meant her world, as in all of it, Maya might have been tempted to think he was crazy, except she had seen him arrive. So she taught him the little she knew. He was older than her, but it didn't matter. In his presence, they were the same. He was wise and did what she believed to be magical, until he explained why it wasn't magic at all. Just a deeper understanding of the forces that held the worlds together. She learned a little of what he meant. Now she wished she had learned more.

Sitting huddled in the car, waiting for the wind to die down, waiting for the answer as to the best thing to do about the arrival from Crann, Maya once again berated herself for not learning enough to free herself and Ginny from Dradon. It had never helped to remind herself that she had been young and foolish about the world, and it didn't help her now either.

Now, alone in the car without a straightforward answer to what to do, Maya wrapped her arms around her legs, knees pulled to her chest and dropped her head to her knees, and waited. For a moment, she thought that if she let herself freeze to death, everyone would be better off. But then Dradon would recognize she did it on purpose, and all this sacrifice would be for nothing.

No, Maya thought. *I have to hope whoever is in there with Ceya and Koda will know what to do. This time I'll listen and do exactly what the three of them ask of me.*

TWENTY THREE

"Mother's Day," the text read. "Are you going to Doveland?"

"Yes! Will you be there?"

She answered with a happy-face Emoji, and Johnny leaned back in his chair and smiled. He would be with Evie in a few days.

They met in the fall when Evie Lynn found her way to Doveland after losing her memory. All she had was a slip of paper with an address on it which turned out to be where her grandfather, Thomas Hendrick, lived.

On her first day of travel, she met James Cahill and Owen Riley when she stopped for food at a pizza shop. Once they realized she had lost her memory and was running away from someone, both of them left their current lives and helped her arrive safely in Doveland. Along the way, they all adopted each other as a family—James as Evie's father, and Owen as her brother.

Once Evie was safe, they all remained in Doveland. James bought a home close to Evie's grandfather, and Thomas and James become part of everyday life in Doveland, while Evie and Owen went off to school. It was a far cry from the lives all of them had lived before. Their story was yet another Doveland transformation.

But to Johnny, something even more magical happened. Evie's coming to Doveland transformed him, too. The moment Johnny saw Evie, he knew Evie was the one for him. However, only after the ordeal ended with her birth father, Leo Gibbons, and his boss, Duke Quinn—both meeting the end they deserved—did Evie allow herself to notice that Johnny was the one for her, too.

But they were both in school and they hadn't seen each other since the Christmas holidays. At least not in person. They used every modern convenience between classes and studying, and even some "magical" ways to keep in touch. But both were looking forward to the real thing!

Yet another reason to love holidays, Johnny thought. They were the perfect excuse to visit family and friends. Although after this year, he wouldn't need that excuse. Johnny had decided that after graduating, he would return to Doveland to live. He would help his mom run her design business while assisting other companies in putting their products and services out in the world. That way he would always be near the ones he loved.

Besides, Doveland was the place he could be himself. He was not the only one who lived there who could do things that most of the world considered strange, weird, or even magical. It was none of that. It was simply an expanded perception of the way the world worked.

Having his gifts meant he was always on call to help others. But in Doveland, he wasn't alone because many people in Doveland lived with that expanded perception.

Although Johnny hadn't enjoyed having his gifts at first, that didn't make them go away. So even though they were often inconvenient and sometimes put him in dangerous situations, they also helped people, which became enough for him.

However, there was another reason he was happy to be heading home. It had been quiet for the last few months, for which he was grateful. But he had a feeling that something was happening. There was nothing specific. No one popped up when he was remote-viewing. And yet, he knew that someone was coming who needed the Doveland Karass' help.

Glancing at the clock, Johnny realized he'd been working at the computer for hours. He needed a break. He stood, stretched, and slipped on his jacket and shoes, not bothering to glance in the mirror. Although still dark, the coffee shop would be open. He'd treat himself to a coffee and then head over to the duck pond to watch the sunrise and listen. Perhaps it would give him an idea of who or what was coming and how he could help.

· · · ● · ● · ● · · ·

While Johnny sat at the duck pond, Ava and her husband Evan discussed the Mother's Day celebration. Their son Ben still slept, so they had a little time to themselves. Like Johnny, they each had coffee in their hands as they sat on the back terrace that faced the forest and the bunkhouse and listened to the morning chorus of birds and frogs. A gravel path lit with tiny lights embedded into the ground led to the bunkhouse.

The two of them ran a private bed-and-breakfast. It used to include the bedrooms in their house, but now they only used the bunkhouse, partially because Ben was older, but also because Evan had converted one bedroom into an office. Ava, thinking then that she wanted her own space, too, converted another bedroom into her office. They kept one guest bedroom in the house, just in case.

The bunkhouse had plenty of room, even though one of the bedrooms belonged permanently to Hank Blaze. He stayed there a few times a week, sometimes to visit, and other times because he was working late and didn't want to go back to his farmhouse outside of Concourse. However, no one was staying at the moment, so the bunkhouse lay dark and silent.

The quiet time with her husband before the sun rose was Ava's favorite time of the day. They had learned the value of this time from their friends, Leif and Sarah, before the two of them left to live elsewhere. But what they had taught them remained.

As they sipped their coffee, Ava and Evan planned the food and the time for the Mother's Day event. Everyone knew the party would be at their house because they designed the house for crowds. It was also the safe house. And they discussed that too. Months had passed since someone had stayed with them for protection. On the one hand, that was a good thing. On the other, to them, it meant that soon the void would be filled, and they wanted to be ready.

As the sun rose, streaming rose gold light through the trees, Ben came outside wrapped in a blanket to sit on his dad's lap. Ava smiled at the sight. The life she lived now was one she could never have imagined, and she felt grateful for every moment. Even the danger that brought them together had made all of them better for overcoming it.

That's why, even though she too knew that something was coming their way, she was more excited than afraid. They all had lived through many adventures together. Whatever came next, they'd get through it together, and everyone would be better off because of it. At least, it had worked that way in the past. She had to have faith it would work that way again.

TWENTY FOUR

As she did every morning as the sun rose, Isira walked to the edge of the cliff and looked down. Far below, she saw the glint of three rivers merging into one.

Isira knew that if she turned around, she would see multiple shades of green as the trees unfurled their spring leaves into a verdant tapestry, sparkling with the morning dew. Some trees came close to the cliff, but between them and the deep forest lay a meadow alive with spring flowers and waving grasses. If she listened closely, she'd hear the stream that ran through her village, providing water for both the residents and the food they grew.

In Crann, nature was the mother of them all, and they treated her with respect and love. The forest was alive within a cycle of life. Trees provided everything their world needed. As a result, they held trees in the highest esteem. Crann was a world of layers, overlapping and entwining.

But Isira knew that was only in her world. If she fell into the next one, most of what she was seeing would not be there. Instead of sounds of waterfalls, streams, wind in the trees, and the calls of the birds, noise would stream from people, cars, trucks, and machines that kept nature at bay.

In the world below, giant machines cut down trees without ever knowing the tree or questioning the wisdom of its removal. The people of Crann knew each tree and asked its permission when they used it. They always left untouched the mother tree and the supporting trees needed to supply the young ones. Machines didn't care. *Neither, apparently,* Isira thought, *did the men running them.*

Isira hated that world. The short time she lived there trying to get Akota and Dradon to come home was absolute torture. She never wanted to be there again. Not that she could go now. Her duty was to stay in Crann. She didn't mind. She was grateful her family dedicated their lives to the good of their people. Throughout many generations, they remained happy, fulfilling their mission. Until Dradon.

Duty was why Akotas returned. Besides, he confided to Isira, he couldn't adjust to the noise and confusion. It was why he didn't follow Maya when she returned to her world to be herself. It broke his heart, but he was confident he made the right decision.

It was different for Dradon. He never felt obligated to the people of his world. Instead, he sought power and used division to get his way. So when Dradon fell into the other world, he felt as if he had found his place.

Dradon loved the noise and clutter and lack of awareness among most of the people. It made them easy to control. He loved the power. He loved everything he couldn't have in Crann. So he stayed and thrived there. And Crann slowly returned to the peace it knew before Dradon made war among the people.

Isira brushed back the strands of dark hair that had escaped the braid that had grown back after all these years, pulled the cloak she wore closer as the wind grew stronger, and sighed. Now Akotas was gone, and she was childless. When she died, there would be no one to care for the people of Crann unless Pax was successful in convincing Akotas' child to leave her world and come to the world of her father. The world she would not have remembered.

To make it worse, they knew nothing about Ginny. She was only a baby the last time they saw her. Would she be capable of doing what needed to be done to keep Crann as it was? Or was she of the other world and would never be happy living away from it? Would she bring greed and corruption with her?

Isira fell to her knees, her forehead resting on the earth, her heavy braid swinging forward, her hands clasped in front of her, and prayed to the God of all that was good asking for the strength and courage to continue on alone and bring joy and harmony to her people. She asked that God give the same strength and courage to Pax.

And she prayed to understand what would be the right thing to do with Dradon. Somehow, he needed to be stopped. But how? Should Pax, Ceya, and Koda return Dradon to Crann, and if they did, what would they do with him? If they let him run free, he would gather his followers together again and declare himself ruler of the land. He would destroy the peace again. And it wouldn't be enough for him. It wasn't enough before, and now that he had tasted the power he had gained in the other world, he would never settle for less.

Would they imprison him? Could they? Would they have to execute him? Could they?

Isira sighed. She knew she couldn't do it, although a part of her hated him and would be happy to take out her vengeance on him. Isira was wise enough to know that she couldn't indulge that part of herself. Because then she would be like him. There were no answers. At least she had no answers. Even though she came to the edge of the cliff every morning and prayed the same prayer, she never received insight into what to do about Dradon.

Akotas said Pax would know what to do, because he had his ancestors' wisdom and courage flowing through him, and he would discover his reservoir of strength in time. Although Isira trusted Akotas, she had not seen in Pax what Akotas claimed Pax to be. Yes, he was the descendant of the one who climbed the cliff, but what did that guarantee?

After all, Dradon was the descendant of a line of leaders who protected the land and the people. And look at him—the exact opposite.

As Isira stood at the cliff, she reached out to her brother Akotas in spirit and begged him to help her, but most of all, help his protege succeed. Akotas might believe in Pax, but Pax needed to believe in himself to do what he needed to do.

Isira bowed once more to the sun as it rose above the horizon and then turned to face the woods. She loved these trees. They had seen all of it—the wars before William Sky and then the peace he brought. As a child, she learned to ask the trees for advice, and the advice she always received was to unite, blend as one, assist those who needed it, and trust in each other.

What else can I do? Isira asked herself. So even though she needed Pax to return with Ginny, she had daily chores and details to handle, and duty was something she understood.

Still, before going to the village, she walked to the tree that stood taller than the clouds. The tree that had been there from the beginning of their world. She leaned into it until the peace it contained flowed into her.

"You can do it, Pax," she whispered, hoping the winds of her world would carry her words to where he was and bring him whatever he needed.

TWENTY FIVE

Koda worried. He had watched and waited all these years, and the person who came to make everything right again was this boy, Pax?

"Are you sure Akotas is right, and Pax is the one?" He asked Ceya more than once. She always responded the same way. Pax would be fine. He was just different.

Koda would nod and smile while clenching his teeth in an effort to agree.

To Koda, teaching Pax was like dealing with a spoiled child, and he didn't like it at all. He couldn't see what Ceya or Akotas had seen in him. Koda understood Ceya had observed Pax his entire life and was used to his independent and stubborn nature, but that was back in Crann. Now, they didn't have time for Pax to question everything and decide if it was what he wanted to do.

What made it even harder was Koda actually liked Pax. He understood the boy tried to do what they asked of him, learn the ways of this world, but he wasn't doing a very good job of it, and his resistance to being told what to do made it worse. Plus, the noise and all the people made Pax even more timid than he had been in Crann.

Privately Ceya also worried. Pax was taking too long to adjust. She often reminded herself how many times Akotas threw up his hands at Pax's determination to do things his way or his withdrawal into himself when he didn't understand or like what was happening.

But, as she told Koda, Pax possessed a good and kind heart. He wanted to do the right thing, he wanted to be part of this solution, but it went against his nature to fight. At first, even crossing the street was an ordeal for him. He didn't want to fight for his place in the crowd or dodge cars. He would wait and wait until she or Koda would push him forward. At one point, Ceya, frustrated with him, whispered to him to use his gift of invisibility and simply walk through the crowd.

He looked at her with such determination that she had stepped back as he said, "No, that is the wrong way to use it."

However, she took heart from his determination to do the right thing. All they needed to do was get him moving in the right direction, so he could exist in this world without flinching every time something he didn't understand happened around him.

The underlying tension of the people around him and the constant threat of violence, whether it was a car coming at him, or people screaming at each other, kept him in a state of continued upset.

"He's a peacemaker," Ceya kept telling Koda. "That's what he's here to do. Bring peace."

"I doubt it, Ceya," Koda finally said, after hearing the excuse one time too many.

"Yes, he is here for a reason, but stopping Dradon? I don't think so. We are going to need help."

"You're right," Ceya finally acknowledged.

Pax had been there a week and was barely functioning in the world. They asked him to learn to be a warrior, and he wasn't, at least not that kind. They needed to admit that although Pax was there to help Ginny and Maya, he, by himself, could not stop Dradon.

"Where will we get help?" Ceya asked Koda.

At that moment, Pax opened the shack's door, having returned from a walk in the park and a sit with the trees. Seeing their faces, he smiled and said, "What have you figured out?"

"That we will need help," Ceya said.

Pax smiled again, opened the door of the shack, and let Maya into the room.

Ceya and Koda gasped and stood as she came towards them with her hands outstretched.

"Thank you for coming, Ceya. And Koda, thank you for watching over me all these years. But now that Pax is here, I want to help."

Ceya paused, ready to lash out, and then realized that Pax had done the right thing. They were the ones who had been dragging their feet, not wanting to approach Maya until he was ready. Well, he was obviously ready in his own way.

Stepping towards Maya, Ceya reached out and pulled her in her arms, feeling how thin she had become.

"Shall we get started?" Pax said. "I'm as ready as I'll ever be and Maya has waited long enough for our help."

Maya smiled at Pax, and Koda understood why Akotas said Pax was the one. Maya immediately trusted him.

"Something is going on with Ginny," Maya said. "She has been seeing someone and not telling me. Of course, that's probably my fault. I have tried so hard to protect her, I have also made it impossible for her to talk to me. But this doesn't feel right."

"Do you know who?" Koda asked.

"No, just that she goes out now when she used to stay home, and she dresses differently."

"Maybe that's a good thing?" Pax said.

"It's not. Ginny can't get involved with someone."

"Why not? What if it makes her happy? Isn't that what you want for her?" Ceya asked.

Maya looked at Ceya and dropped her head.

"She doesn't know who she is, does she?"

Maya shook her head, tears gathering in her eyes. "No. I never told her. How could I explain Akotas, another world, and her part in it? Especially since I didn't know when, or if, someone would come to help, and Dradon's threats have ruled my life. I shouldn't even be here with you. If he finds out, he'll hurt her."

"Why? Why does he bother with you? Why not leave you alone?" Pax asked.

"Because he knows Ginny would be the next High Priestess of Crann. If she ever gets there," Koda said.

"And why would he care about that? He has the power he wants here."

"You don't know Dradon," Maya whispered. "He has always planned to return to Crann and turn it into a world like this one. Dradon knows that even if he gets rid of Isira and Akotas, if the people find out about Ginny, they won't accept him. Although he might enjoy the war it would cause, it would be much easier to get rid of everyone else in his family. Ginny is in his way. However, if she doesn't know who she is, I thought she would be safe."

Pax leaned back in his chair, thinking about what Maya had said. There had to be a reason Dradon kept Ginny and Maya around. It would have been easier to just get rid of them. Probably Maya knew why but didn't feel safe telling them yet.

But first, they had to make sure Ginny was safe, so he asked, "How does Dradon track what you do and know? What powers does he have?"

TWENTY SIX

The subject of their discussion was enjoying himself as he admired the view from the penthouse of one of the many buildings he owned. Dradon Good stood at the floor-to-ceiling windows and looked out over the world he loved spread below him. He loved it all.

Streets and highways threaded their way through buildings of all shapes and sizes. Lights from cars, streetlights, and buildings blazed brighter than any star in the sky. In the distance, he could see the glint of the three rivers as the sun rose. They were the same three rivers in his old world. The boring one. The one he would change when he went back to it. It was time. He was ready.

There were only a few details to manage first. He needed to make sure Akotas' offspring never made it to Crann to claim the role of High Priestess.

He made his mark in this world, ruling over people the same way he would rule over the people of Crann. But no matter how successful he became, he would never rule the entire world. There were far too many other people like him in this world. He had observed with grudging respect how they built their businesses, took what they wanted for themselves, and fooled others into thinking they cared.

He even merged his business with some of them. Then, when they weren't looking, he took over what they'd built. Their greed blinded them. But not everyone succumbed to his tactics. Some were smart enough to see what he was doing, and others didn't need him.

No matter how ruthless he became, he remained the newcomer. They were born into families that had ruled for many generations, just as his family had in Crann. But in this world, they were called the titans of industry, not caretakers. Many of them ruled behind the scenes, and only a selected few were aware of what they did.

They might have allowed Dradon into some of their circles, but he would never be one of them. As much as Dradon wanted to ruin them, he realized he didn't stand a chance. If he'd been born in one of those families, then perhaps it would have worked. But Dradon realized that as successful as he had become in the relatively short time he had been in this world, he was nearing the limit of how much of the world he could control.

It was time to return to Crann and do what he always intended to do. Change it to fit himself and the life he loved. And that was why he kept Maya and her brat, Ginny, alive. Not because he made them some promise. Only fools made promises, and even greater fools believed them. They only fooled themselves, like Maya.

That Maya believed him gave him great pleasure as he watched her shut down her life to keep her daughter safe. No, he had kept them alive, not because he promised her but for himself, as he did everything. Now that he was ready to return to Crann, the time had come to deal with them. Maya for what she knew, and Ginny because of what she was and didn't know.

Dradon checked his watch, so fancy he still hadn't yet figured out how to use many of its functions. He expected Fred to check in soon. Fred told him Ginny knew nothing about her heritage or her dual citizenship and the power it gave her. She knew nothing about Crann or her father. She did not know that she was the only one who belonged to both worlds.

Maya had kept her promise not to tell. She was a fool. It wouldn't save either of them. But first, he needed Maya's secret. Then, now that he was ready, he would return to Crann and take over.

It would be more manageable now. He wouldn't need to fight like a savage. He was so much more aware of how to find the thread of fear and selfishness that ran through everyone and pull on it until people did his bidding. Even Maya, who should have known better. He had pulled her thread of fear, and she had effectively been his prisoner all these years.

Yes, it was time to go home. He only had one minor problem. Even though he searched for it, he had not found the cliff he, Akotas, and Isira fell from. Until he found the cliff or portal back to Crann, he couldn't return. And that was the only reason he had allowed Maya to live. She had to know how to go through the portal without climbing a cliff. That was something he could not do. Climb the cliff? No, he would never make it. As far as he knew, only one person ever made the journey that way. The cliff climber. The one who brought peace to Crann.

Dradon knew there must be another way to return. Akotas had taken Maya to Crann. They couldn't have climbed the cliff. Isira must also know how to return to Crann. How did they both know and not him? He dared not think of how angry that made him. It clouded his thinking. It didn't matter anyway. Once he got Maya to reveal the secret she kept, he would return and make his version of peace.

When he first fell off the cliff and found a world full of cities and noise, he never wanted to go back. Isira tried to get the two of them to return with her before the two months ran out. But neither of them wanted to. He wanted to stay and conquer the world he found himself in, and Akotas wished to remain because he had found love.

Love, Dradon snorted. *What use was that?* He could buy all the love he wanted. He could have any pleasures of this world at any time. And once he was back in Crann, he would have the pleasures of both worlds.

But first, he had to get Maya to show him the way. That would be easy. He controlled her daughter now. After that, he would need to get rid of them both. Maya, because she knew the secret, and Ginny, before she found out.

TWENTY SEVEN

Ginny thought Fred's smile was charming. In fact, she had to admit to herself that she thought all of Fred was charming. He was soft-spoken, kind, and thoughtful. It was as if he was filling up a hole in her that had existed all her life, the need to be seen and then cared about. It was what she tried to do for her children. Give them what they were missing. Some of them only needed a little attention or encouragement. But others needed to be reminded every day that they were loved and cared for, at least by her.

She gave them what her mother didn't seem capable of giving to her. She recognized her mother loved her, but it wasn't enough. The touch of a hand, an interesting conversation, a level gaze that looked straight at her and saw her, that's what she was missing. And Fred was doing all of that for her.

Yes, she knew it had only been a week since he had come to the school to check it out for his little girl. Since then, they'd gone to dinner together almost every evening. She dressed carefully every morning, knowing she'd see him later, avoiding her mother's questions about where she was going after school.

So far, it had just been dinner and conversation, which was fine with her. That was enough to make her happy, and a romance with all the attachments didn't interest her. She hoped it didn't interest Fred. At least not for a little while.

Ginny wanted to meet his daughter, Rose. But Fred said she was finishing up school where they had been living and staying with his mother and father.

He showed her a picture of his daughter, and she said she looked exactly like him. He said no, Rose had her mother's eyes. It broke Ginny's heart when Fred told the story of how his wife died of complications from the birth, and he'd been a single parent ever since, with the help of his parents, of course, for whom he was very grateful.

Today he was taking her to his favorite restaurant. The excitement fueled her day with the children, and even they asked her why she looked different. She wanted to say it was because she felt seen, but she didn't. Not because they wouldn't understand. Because one thing she knew about children is that they understood much more than people expected they did. No, it was because somewhere inside her it felt wrong to be important to someone, maybe even loved. It was easier to believe that she wasn't deserving, which is why her mother avoided her.

Maybe her father was a wicked man, and every time her mother looked at her, she saw that person. She wouldn't know, since her mother told her nothing about her father. She must have loved him, though. After all, she kept his cracked mirror in the hallway.

No, Ginny told herself. She didn't believe it was because her mother didn't love her father. It was for some other reason that she avoided Ginny. It didn't matter, anyway. She was thinking too much about this. She and Fred were friends. That was enough for now. But eventually, she would have to tell her mother because it was the right thing to do. She was not looking forward to it.

On the other hand, her mother had been acting differently for the past few days. More prolonged glances, a pause before she went out the door as if she wanted to say something. Perhaps she already knew Ginny was seeing someone?

Ginny sighed as she turned to help one of her students tuck in his shirt. Patting him on the top of his head, she scooted him into the room so she could begin the day. Yes, it was probably time to tell her mom about Fred. It probably wouldn't go well, but she was tired of being a nobody and not standing up for herself. Fred was the first step to independence. It was time to live her life.

· · ● · ● · ● · ● · ● ·

It hadn't taken long for Fred to see precisely how to gain Ginny's trust. His make-believe daughter was the key, along with quietly listening and making Ginny feel heard and cared for. Adjusting his more abrasive, although quiet personality, to what would make Ginny feel safe was easy for him. He had always either blended in or completely disappeared within groups, just as he intended.

The problem was, he was making up more and more of a story as Ginny continued to ask about his daughter. He had to invent loving parents along with a beautiful daughter. He finally wrote out an entire story about his make-believe life for himself to make sure he didn't deviate from it when he talked to Ginny.

He had to admit to himself that Ginny was a nice girl. It was her downfall, and it suited his purposes. He wanted to stay close to her, and he would not ruin it by turning it into a romantic relationship that could so quickly go wrong. His mission was all that counted—get rid of Dradon and take over his business. Although he didn't understand why he knew somehow Ginny was the key.

Dradon wanted Fred to watch her, but he was going to do more than that. He would find out what was behind Dradon's power and use that against him. Sticking close to Ginny would reveal that secret to him. It didn't hurt that he enjoyed being with her, and he ignored the part of himself that reminded him she might not survive his plan.

TWENTY EIGHT

To Johnny's deep disappointment, Evie decided not to return to Doveland for Mother's Day. Instead, her grandfather and James were coming to spend the weekend with her and Owen.

He understood. Evie had a new life to make for herself, and although both of them believed they would eventually make a life together, she wasn't ready. At first, Johnny said he would come to Evie, but when he felt her silence over the phone, he knew that was the wrong thing for both of them.

She wanted alone time with her newly found family, and he had to return to Doveland. It was not only to be with his mother on Mother's Day but also because whoever was coming their way was much closer. Despite having not remote-viewed anyone, he was positive that something was happening. To make sure he would be in Doveland when it did, he arranged with his professors to do the rest of his classes online. There were only a few weeks left in the semester anyway.

The day before he left, he walked around the campus, mentally saying goodbye. Thanks to a member of the Doveland Karass, they had a condo that anyone could come and stay in when they wanted to, so he wasn't saying goodbye forever. He was only saying goodbye to being a student. He was saying goodbye to the boy who came to school to find his way after learning about his father's association with the town's doctor, who had turned out to be a serial killer.

In his first year in school, Johnny tried to come to grips with his gifts that set him apart from everyone. He could read their minds if he wanted to. He didn't want to and used that skill only in emergencies. He could remote-view people, but it only happened when they were a danger to his family and friends.

He was grateful that all his gifts appeared to be ones that helped others stay safe and otherwise left him alone so he could live an ordinary life. Or at least allow him to appear normal, even though he wasn't.

So going home to Doveland would mean not only that he had grown enough to be himself—without worrying if he would be like his father, too weak to say no to evil—but also that he would be among others like himself.

In the past, he had surprised his mother on Mother's Day, but this year, she knew he was coming. Throwing the last of his possessions into his car, Johnny took one last drive as a student through the streets that he loved and then turned his car toward home, wondering what adventure was waiting for him there.

• • • • ● • ● • • • •

"Are you ready, Pax?" Koda asked.

Pax didn't know what to say. Was he ready? As always, everything felt as if it was moving too quickly. How could he be ready? He didn't belong in this world. None of it made sense to him. Why was it so noisy? Why did people rush around so much?

Why were there so few trees? Didn't people realize that trees made the world that they lived in?

He had asked these questions, and many more of Koda, Ceya, and Maya. Even Maya, who lived in this world, who had chosen it over Crann, had no answers. Pax felt separated from all that he loved and could not see how he would ever feel whole again until he returned home.

Except now that he was on this mission, he had to complete it. Otherwise, he would return home and still not be whole. He couldn't change the world, but he could do something to help Maya and her daughter.

"One thing at a time," Koda kept saying to him. "Just move forward. We're here to help."

Sure, Pax thought, *easy for you to say.*

But Pax knew it was time to take the next step. Maya and Ceya were waiting outside for him. The two of them were restless, but Maya was almost jumping out of her skin waiting for him.

Maya returned to the shack that morning, looking as if she was ready to set the world on fire. The day before, she followed Ginny after school and watched as Ginny met a man for dinner, laughing and giggling the way she had when she was just a child.

Maya had been torn between loving to hear her daughter laugh and terrified that she was losing her just when it was time to rescue her. Of course, Ginny didn't realize she needed rescuing. All she probably knew was that someone was making her happy. Finally.

All night Maya lay awake. She heard Ginny come home, apparently right after dinner, but that gave her only a momentary sense of comfort. Eventually, Ginny would fall in love with someone and leave her. Leave her destiny. The one she knew nothing about.

Whose fault is that? Maya kept asking herself. She should have never left Crann. She should have told Ginny who her father was and what that meant for her future. She shouldn't have been so willful and such a coward at the same time.

So by the time morning came, Maya was both exhausted and determined. So determined that she had made herself smile at Ginny, which made Ginny ask if there was something wrong. Wasn't this backward? Her smiling shouldn't mean there was a problem. But after all these years of scowling apparently it was.

"No," Maya managed to say. "But if I come home early from work today, could we talk?"

"Talk?" Ginny almost shouted, thinking how long she had wished that they could talk, and now that she had someone to talk to, her mother wanted to talk? Now?

Ginny thought about her date with Fred after school and how much she was looking forward to seeing him. But her mother never asked for anything. She would call him and reschedule. He would understand how important it was for her to meet with her mother.

Maya almost resorted to pleading when finally Ginny nodded and said yes.

"Shall we meet at the cafe near the park?" Maya asked.

Ginny said okay, and then while driving off, wondered how in the world her mother knew about the cafe near the park. Ginny was both delighted and upset that her mother wanted to talk. But mostly, she was curious about why.

So when she called Fred to tell him she couldn't meet him after school, and he said he understood, but asked what was going on, Ginny took the time to tell him where she was going and why she was curious.

Fred paused before saying, "Sounds great. Have a good time. We'll meet tomorrow, instead."

Ginny, smiling, hung up and hummed to herself as she hugged each child in her classroom. Life was getting much better.

Ginny was the only one who thought so.

Pax, waiting to go with Ceya, Maya, and Koda to the cafe, didn't think so. Fred, who knew something had changed, didn't think so, and when he reported to Dradon, Dradon's fury told him that his life was about to get worse if he didn't figure out what was going on and stop it.

The question was how.

TWENTY NINE

They arrived at the cafe only a few minutes before Ginny was due to be there. Maya was in a tizzy. She wanted to be there long before Ginny, giving herself time to get calm, and to think through, once again, what she was going to say to her daughter.

How would she explain something she barely understood herself? Would Ginny believe the story that Maya saw a man fall from another world, fell in love with him, married, and had Ginny? That she and Akotas returned to his world where she learned he was part of the family considered the keepers of the peace of that world?

How could she explain Crann and that although it was another dimension of this world, it was so different she couldn't adjust? How could she justify leaving Akotas and bringing Ginny back to this world only to be held a prisoner in her own life by Dradon?

Every way she looked at the story she had to tell, it all sounded crazy. It's why she was grateful she would not tell the story by herself. Perhaps Ginny would listen to the others. They were going to leave the part out that Koda and Ceya were hawks. That would be one detail too many. Actually, there were many details Maya intended to leave out in this first telling of the story to Ginny.

Yes, Maya had hoped she could sit quietly and prepare herself for Ginny's arrival and find the best way to tell her a story that would change her life forever. But Pax and his constant dragging of his feet made them late, and she had no time. She was not happy.

Koda and Ceya weren't happy either. They wanted to arrive early enough to have Pax adjust to his surroundings. They knew what he was like in public. They wanted time for him to get used to the chatter of the surrounding people. To hold a cup of tea as if he was used to it, instead of constantly peering inside as if he was looking for real leaves, or maybe twigs, like the tea he was used to having in Crann.

Pax had tried coffee again and still hating it spit it out on the floor. They had to make excuses for his inappropriate behavior in public. So they settled on a herbal tea with a faint hint of something familiar. They needed Pax to look as normal as possible, so his appearance and manner of being wouldn't put off Ginny. But they knew even wearing the right clothes and drinking tea the right way, there was something about him that made people look. Koda and Ceya were skilled at adjusting themselves to fit into this world. They'd been here before. They didn't like this world much better than Pax did, but at least they were better at pretending than Pax.

Pax wasn't happy either, because he was too scared to feel anything other than worry. What if he did everything wrong? Pax realized he disappointed Koda and Ceya, and maybe even Maya. Perhaps they expected him to be a warrior, and he wasn't. Not physically, and not in his heart.

He yearned to be back among the trees and the clouds. He disliked everything around him. The tea that certainly wasn't tea. The restrictive clothes. The artificial light in the room. The noise of the coffee maker. The chatter about nothing.

Only the quiet people sitting at a table typing on what he had learned was a computer which connected people to the entire world didn't annoy him, although he couldn't understand why they needed a machine to do that. In his world, within his trees, he was always connected to his world.

But he was determined to do what he had come to do. Help Ginny and Maya, release Maya from Dradon's hold, and convince Ginny they needed her in Crann. That seemed impossible to Pax, but he trusted Isira and Akotas, and they were positive he could do it. He had to hold on to that because he knew Ceya and Koda had doubts. He couldn't blame them for that. He had doubts, too.

By the time Maya ordered for everyone, and the four of them settled themselves around the table, it was time for Ginny to arrive. Maya sat where Ginny would see her first. She knew it was weird enough to be there in the first place, but to have three strangers sitting with her was going to make Ginny at least a little nervous. But that couldn't be helped. The four of them had discussed multiple ways to introduce the three people from Crann to Ginny and had decided on this way.

They agreed that the story they would tell Ginny could range from slightly true, to not true at all, to the whole truth. They were going to gauge Ginny's reaction to meeting them and go from there. Ceya would do most of the talking. Their entire aim was to meet, set up another meeting, and do it so casually perhaps Dradon would think nothing of it if he was watching. Which they had to assume he was.

All of them understood that once they started talking to Ginny, they had to be prepared to leave. It would be wonderful if Ginny immediately agreed to return to Crann, but that was so unlikely they had another plan. They would all go into hiding. They knew where to go. It was where Isira had told Pax to go before he had dropped off the cliff, a town where there were people who could help them.

The four of them ran various scenarios of how to get Ginny to listen to them, believe them, and then leave with them. Koda said they would make it work. But first, Ginny needed to show up.

THIRTY

F red stood outside of the school, waiting for Ginny to leave. He had his coat collar turned up against the spring wind. White petals from the poplar tree were blowing across the school front lawn, and some children waiting for the bus twirled around like the petals giggling and laughing. He saw a small skinny boy standing by himself in the shadows of the trees, watching the laughter, and felt as if he was looking at himself.

He understood exactly what that boy was feeling. He wanted to reach out and whisper in his ear that he would be alright and that perhaps now was the time for pretending to be a flower petal before life got too serious. Fred caught the boy's eye and tilted his head towards the laughing, twirling children, whispering to himself, "Go join them."

The boy stared at Fred, looked at the children, and then dropped his gaze to the ground. Fred shook his head and then turned back to watch for Ginny, whispering again, "You should have listened, kid," to himself as much as to the boy who now stood at the back of the line waiting to board the bus.

The boy turned to look at Fred once more before stepping onto the bus. Fred knew what the kid saw. Nothing encouraging.

Just some little, skinny, balding man wearing a nice coat. Maybe even the kid thought he was a pervert. He shook off the feelings of regret. He could do nothing more for that kid. He had to concentrate on what he was there to do. Stop Ginny from going to the meeting.

She wasn't looking for him as she came out holding the hand of one of her students, her head bent down to hear what the little girl was saying, a smile on her face as she listened. He watched her hand the girl to her mother, then, pulling her coat tighter around her, head down, she headed for her car.

"Ginny," he called, hurrying after her.

Startled, she looked up, saw him, and it pleased him that she smiled. Fred let his face look as worried as he felt and said again, "Ginny."

She waited as he rushed up to her, reached out and grabbed both her hands, and then letting his voice catch just the slightest bit, because too much and she would be suspicious knowing his stoic nature, he said, "I need your help."

Ginny paled. "What's wrong?"

"It's my daughter."

"What? What about your daughter?"

"She didn't make it to school today."

"Wait, what?" Ginny said, taking Fred's hand and directing him to the bench at one of the bus stops. All the children had left for the day. Fred thought it was just like Ginny not to leave school until all the children were safe. Now he was telling her that his daughter wasn't safe. It was the perfect story to tell.

Fred dropped his head and allowed himself to shiver. Ginny put her arm across his back and leaned in. For a moment, he understood how her students must feel.

"Tell me what's going on, Fred."

Ginny knew her mother was waiting for her. It was the first time in as long as she could remember that her mother wanted to meet and talk. She needed to be there. She couldn't be late. But here was Fred, suffering. And where was his daughter? She knew she had to find out what was happening. She had to help.

"Tell me what you mean. What about your daughter?"

"Mom and Dad called. The school called them and said Rose never arrived at school. She never even got on the bus."

"Didn't your parents wait at the bus stop with her?"

"It stops at the end of their driveway. It's in a quiet neighborhood. Everyone watches out for everyone else, so they never thought it wasn't safe. Rose is used to getting on the bus by herself. She goes out only a few minutes before it comes, so she is never standing there long."

"Didn't the bus driver stop?"

Fred realized he was telling a story to someone who would ask all the right questions, and he was going to have to make up more of a story than he intended to.

"I believe it was a new driver. The kids said Rose was always there, so if she wasn't there, it was because she wasn't coming, so he drove on."

In the back of Ginny's mind, she wondered about what kind of bus driver wouldn't honk and wait before driving on and how could a young girl disappear within minutes right outside her own house, but Fred was so upset, she put those questions aside. She would get to the irresponsibility of the people involved later. Right now, Fred didn't need to hear that. He needed to know it was going to be okay. But she knew it might not be.

The horrors of what could happen to Fred's daughter flashed through her mind before she said, "What can I do to help?"

"The police are there, but I need to go and do something myself. I know you have an important meeting with your mother, but your insight into children would be so helpful. Maybe you would see something no one else would."

Still holding Fred's hand, feeling how sweaty it was, thinking about how she would feel if she had a daughter and she was missing, Ginny wondered what to do. How would her mother feel if she canceled the first and only time she had ever asked to meet her after school?

Ginny sighed and dropped her head. She had waited her entire life to have a mother who spoke with her. This was the opening she had been waiting for. But which was more important? Her wishes, her mother's feelings, or a missing child. It was possible she could help. She didn't know how, but at the same time, she didn't know how not to try.

Turning back to Fred, who reminded her once more of a lost puppy, she asked, "What exactly do you want me to do?"

"Could you come with me? Help me find her?"

Ginny nodded, her heart sinking with the thoughts of her mother, but knowing it was possible that she could help find Rose.

Fred stood, gathered Ginny in his arms and whispered, "Thank you," in her ear, and felt her tremble in response.

"Come," he said, "I'll drive."

Ginny looked at her car and felt a deep desire to get in her car instead of Fred's and head towards her mother. But then, seeing his urgent and pale face, she simply said, "Okay. Let me call my mother."

"Thank you, thank you," Fred said, pulling her towards the car. He knew the school cameras would catch what he was doing, so he was careful to make sure it looked like Ginny was coming of her own free will. Which, of course, she was.

"You can call her in the car. I'm so worried. Can we hurry?"

Ginny nodded and slinging her purse over her shoulder, rushed with him to the car. He opened the car door for her. She slid in, and as he reached across to help buckle her in, pretending that the seat belt was stuck, lifted her phone from her coat pocket and put it into his.

As he crossed behind the car, he dropped it behind his car wheel, and as Fred pulled out, he was careful to reverse first. Hearing the crunch of the phone, he smiled to himself.

The object of Dradon's desire was in his car. And in his care. Which was where she was going to stay.

THIRTY ONE

"**S**he's not coming," Maya said, with a flat voice. She had so many emotions rolling around inside of her, she couldn't let any of them come out. Otherwise, she knew she would fall apart. She had to go back to being the woman without emotions, the one that lived a life of the dead while living. She wasn't sure she could do that anymore.

She had kept herself in line all these years. She kept her self-imposed rules so that Ginny could be happy. Well, not self-imposed. They were Dradon rules, but she had kept them.

And look at where it had gotten them, she moaned inside herself. Ginny, her beloved. The one thing that was important in her life was not coming. She had failed at everything. The contempt Maya felt for herself was so overwhelming she wished she would stop breathing. Die right then and there. What was the point of going on? She had failed. Her daughter wasn't coming. She had chosen not to come. Maya was sure that Ginny had decided to see her new friend Fred instead. She didn't know why, but it didn't matter. And then Maya realized perhaps it did matter. Maybe she wasn't coming because she couldn't come.

The moan she had been keeping inside escaped, filling the entire space of the coffee shop. Everyone turned to look. She didn't care. She couldn't stop.

It was Pax who stood, pulled Maya to her feet, and, gathering her in his arms, led her outside to a bench under the one tree on the block.

Ceya and Koda looked at each other, both of them thinking the same thing—what Maya must have realized. Ginny wasn't coming because someone was stopping her, and perhaps Pax was the right person for this mission after all.

• • • ● • ● • ● • • •

"I knew I'd find you here," Johnny said, winding his way through the tables at Your Second Home to reach his mother.

Valerie had stood and opened her arms to welcome her son home by the time he reached her table. After hugging his mother, Johnny turned to Grace and hugged her, too. He was so happy to be home, he turned around and said, "Anyone else want to hug?"

The few people in the cafe laughed, stood, and hugged everyone they could reach, most of them making their way to Johnny before sitting back down again, smiling at the spontaneous outpouring of community hugging.

No one was surprised. It was Doveland. Johnny, still standing, bowed and smiled at each table before sitting down with his mother and Grace, overjoyed at being home. And then it hit him. He was home. To stay this time. And he smiled again, thinking of how much he had changed. From the boy who felt so alone he acted out, to what he realized he was now—a young man who knew what he wanted and was happy with himself and his world.

Grace watched Johnny, thinking how much she loved this young man. It wasn't as if she didn't find love in her heart for everyone, but watching Johnny grow up these last few years had helped her heart heal after her husband, Eric, had died. She'd always miss him, but she knew they would meet again, and wherever he was, he was doing good as he had while they were together. They had little time together, but they had made the most of it.

"Are you two planning something?" Johnny asked once he had gotten his coffee and a scone. Grace had suggested he try one, and after he moaned with pleasure about how delicious it was, Grace told him that Lex had made them. He was trying his hand at pastries, along with continuing with Pete's cooking class.

"He's quite talented, your brother," Grace said.

Valerie beamed.

Johnny put down his cup and asked, "Has Lex done any more remote-viewing?"

"Not that I know about," Valerie said, glancing at Grace. She knew that sometimes Lex came to Grace first, both her boys thinking of Grace as their grandmother. She couldn't blame them. Grace was the perfect woman to go to for anything. And her boys were not the only children who thought of Grace that way.

"He hasn't said anything."

Johnny looked at both women and realized there was something else going on. Something more than two friends having coffee together.

"What's happening?"

When neither one of them responded, Johnny added, "You're not fooling me by being quiet. You two are up to something, and don't tell me it's all about planning some event."

"We are planning an event," Grace laughed. "Mother's Day at Ava and Evan's."

"And, what else," Johnny said.

Grace turned to Valerie and said, "Might as well tell him he's going to bug us until we do."

"What!" Johnny demanded.

Valerie smiled at her son and said, "Grace had a visitor."

"Good lord, mom, that means nothing. Grace always has visitors. She's practically the entire town's hostess."

"It wasn't someone who lives here."

Impatient now, Johnny lowered his voice and said, "Tell me the story straight. Leave nothing out."

THIRTY TWO

Ginny put her head back on the headrest of Frank's car, closed her eyes, and silently wept within. *I will not show any emotion,* she promised herself. But inside, she pinged-ponged between rage and sadness. She was a complete and total idiot. She knew it now. But she wouldn't give Fred the pleasure or the control of knowing how she was feeling.

Instead, she calmed herself and asked, "Tell me more about Rose. Could she have gone off with a friend? What is she interested in? Is it possible that she is just playing hooky? Kids do that sometimes, you know."

Fred turned and smiled at Ginny. If she wanted to play this game, he was happy to do so. The only part he didn't like about it was that he needed to make up a story about some little girl. He didn't like kids. He never had. Sure, he knew himself well enough to understand it was because he had been so bullied as a child. Big deal. It didn't mean he had to learn to like them.

But here he was making up a kid called Rose. The name had popped into his head and out of his mouth before he could take it back. It was his mother's middle name. Joline Rose Stiles. So as he made up things about a little girl that didn't exist, he pictured his mother as she might have been when she was young.

Ginny listened intently to his story. Now that she realized he was making it up, she hoped the story would give her some way to control Fred, or at least influence him in her favor. She wouldn't underestimate him again. But she needed more information about who he was and why he had kidnapped her. Because that was what was going on, even though they were pretending it wasn't.

As they had driven away from the parking lot, she had reached into her coat pocket for her phone. It wasn't there, so she started digging through her purse, looking for it. Perhaps she had dropped it in there without thinking about it.

Fred had asked her what she was looking for.

"My phone," Ginny had answered, experiencing the edge of panic. She reached under her seat and then tried to turn around in case it had slipped out of her pocket, onto the floor, and was now in the back. But she couldn't. Her seatbelt kept her from turning. So she tried unlatching it. It wouldn't. She was stuck in her seat.

Still not realizing what was happening, she asked Fred for help.

"Are you stuck?" Fred asked, smiling.

It was the smile that gave him away. It didn't reach his eyes.

"Sorry about that. Sometimes it sticks. I'll fix it when we get to my parents' house."

"But my mother. I need to call my mother right now."

"She'll be okay. We'll call her soon. You realize I have to find Rose. Think about me, Ginny. Give it a rest."

It all sounded perfectly normal. Ginny might have bought the story for a little longer if it hadn't been for the weird smile. But the feeling she had before stepping into the car came back in a rush.

How many times had her mother told her to be careful? How many times had she taught her children not to get into a car with a stranger? And yet, she had not been careful or followed her own rules. Fred was a stranger. She didn't know him at all.

It was then that she had laid her head back on the seat, trying not to show the turmoil of emotions raging inside her. She still had a chance. If she could fool him into making him think she still believed him, she had a chance.

So she asked him about Rose and listened to his story with a growing appreciation for his ability to tell stories, along with increasing respect for her mother. Somehow, these two things were connected.

Her mother had been acting differently for the last few days. A little lighter, perhaps. She had even seen her stand in front of the cracked mirror and reach out and touch its battered frame with such tenderness Ginny had felt jealous. Of a mirror, of all things.

And then she had invited Ginny to meet with her at a cafe. How had she missed how important that was? When she chose Fred's daughter over her mother, was she punishing her, or was she just an idiot, ignoring all the signs. Helping the wrong person, and now in some trouble. She had to find out why.

Ginny was sure of one thing. This was not a random event. Fred had targeted her. Her mother had protected her in her own way, but from what? She'd find out. She was used to pretending. She could fool Fred.

So as Fred made up a story about a daughter that didn't exist, and Ginny listened as if she worried about the little girl, Fred celebrated. This was easier than he thought it was going to be. He was sure Ginny had figured out that he had kidnapped her, but instead of resisting, she acted as if everything was okay.

It made things easier for him to drive. But once they stopped, he would have to restrain her because he knew Ginny would try to get away. It would not happen. He had what Dradon wanted, and he was going to use her to find out what he needed to know to take over Dradon's businesses. Dradon could stay as the figurehead if he could control him. Otherwise, he would replace him with another figurehead.

Fred didn't want or enjoy the limelight. He enjoyed being the quiet man who ran everything, with only a few people knowing. It would be up to Dradon whether or not he kept his life. Fred suspected Dradon would not give in. But first, he had to find out why Ginny was so important to Dradon before he could take Dradon's power away.

In the meantime, he would play along with this woman. She was beautiful and intelligent. If things were different, he might even let himself like her. But he couldn't. He had bigger plans, and no person, even this lovely woman, would ruin them.

So he continued with the story about Rose. He made up stories about who she was and how much he worried about her, as if she was real and as if he cared. And Ginny played along.

Ginny didn't know why it was happening, but she was determined that Fred would not keep her from her mother and what she wanted to tell her. How she would get away, she didn't know. But there was one thing Ginny knew for sure. Her life would never be the same, and a small piece of her was glad. Whatever the secret was that her mother kept from her all these years would come out in the open, and she was ready for it.

While both Ginny and Fred plotted out their plans, neither knew that there was much more at stake than they could imagine. Neither of them realized they were pawns in a game that would determine the fate of at least one world and the direction of another.

THIRTY THREE

All his life Dradon had expected to be treated like royalty. Because he was. The title of High Priest and High Priestess had been in their family for many generations. It was a title given to them by the man who climbed the cliff.

After leading the people of Crann into a time of peace, William Sky said that there would always need to be an overseer for the people. The people would need to know and believe that the welfare of their world was always in safe hands, that there would always be someone watching over them, someone who would put the people's interest ahead of their own. William Sky called those people the High Priest and High Priestess, but only with the understanding that they, and their offspring, would always continue the work of keeping the peace in Crann.

He chose Dradon's ancestors as that family because they were the ones who protected him when he first arrived. They kept him safe against the rebels who wanted no part of peace. There were many people upset about the ending of wars. Wars allowed them to rule, to be in control for themselves and not for the good of their world. And they were willing to fight to have it. It took many, many trips around the sun before almost all the people of Crann chose peace.

They kept those that still wanted to fight in one small village, isolated from everyone else. A group of people called The Protectors watched over them.

Over the centuries, the number of people in that village declined, and peace and cooperation became the accepted way of life.

But then I came along, Dradon chucked to himself. *A misfit from the start.*

Dradon was a disappointment to his parents, someone for his siblings to fear, and then eventually all of Crann to fear. He went to the village, gathered the few remaining misfits, helped them kill The Protectors, who had grown careless, and then led the misfits against the rest of Crann. He was their ruler. They fought against all that his family stood for. Dradon brought back war. He named his warriors Satoka after his brother Akotas. He knew when Akotas figured out it was his name in reverse, it would break his heart. Dradon loved every minute of the fighting, but it was too easy. He wanted more. Falling off the cliff came at the perfect time.

Now, after all this time, Dradon knew his family would still be the caretakers of a peaceful Crann. Akotas and Isira would have done what was required of them to contain those that wanted to fight. It would have been easy since Dradon, their ruler, was no longer there.

The world that he fell into had already been at war. Insurrections of all sizes were common. People fought within families. Dividing lines existed everywhere. With all the separation and contentions between people, Dradon found it easy to become the ruler of one company after another. It was easier than using physical weapons and fighting in the street. Rule a company. Rule a world. It was easy to turn people against each other in this world.

However, it all bored him now. He couldn't rise higher than he had already risen. There were too many other people like him. Although he was accepted into most of their elite circles, he could never be the ruler of the entire world.

The desire to return to Crann and turn it into a world like this one, but where he would become and remain the one and only ruler, burned within him. He wouldn't be the High Priest of Peace. No. He, Dradon, would be the One Ruler of Crann. He could easily overthrow his brother and sister if they were still alive. He would destroy their children, starting with Ginny once he was finished with her.

Dradon already knew precisely how to transform Crann into his image. This world had taught him so much control. He had used brute force before, and although that had its place, he was older and wiser now. Now he knew what to do. He would destroy the forests and then the land. And he would control the little land left to grow food.

He would separate people. There would be no nightly gatherings in village centers to watch the sun go down and discuss the day. He would spread rumors about people, make some better than others. Divide and conquer was his motto in business, and it was exactly how he would go about controlling Crann.

It was frustrating not to know what was going on in Crann now, so he could plan better. But what infuriated him was that he couldn't figure out how to return. Somehow Maya knew how. And perhaps her daughter. Ginny was the key. If he controlled her, Maya would have to tell him how to go back.

It was the only reason they were both still alive. Dradon knew someday he would be ready to return, and that time had come. He was a small ruler here in this world, but he would be the only ruler in his homeworld.

Dradon glanced at his watch. It was past the time for Fred to check in. Not for the first time, Dradon sensed a twinge of worry about Fred. However, in the past, he had convinced himself that Fred was what he appeared to be. His right-hand man. Efficient and capable. A follower, not a leader. But now, realizing that he was ready to return to Crann, Dradon let that pang of worry grow. What if he'd been wrong about Fred? And Fred had Ginny—the key to his future success.

Just then, his phone rang. He answered, not saying anything, letting his silence speak his displeasure at Fred's lateness.

"Sorry, sir," Fred said. He knew enough not to offer an excuse for being late checking in.

Dradon continued the silence a moment longer before asking, "Yes?"

Fred understood what he meant. "Yes," he said. "All is well."

Dradon said nothing more. He hung up, put both hands on his desk, dropped his head, and breathed deeply. Something was wrong. It was time to find out what it was.

Fred listened to the phone's silence for a few seconds before putting the phone down and looking over at Ginny, who smiled at him as if they were a couple.

She's good, Fred thought and smiled back at her. *But not as good as me. Both she and Dradon are about to find out who I really am.*

His smile broadened at the thought, and Ginny, observing him, felt as if she was looking at a snake getting ready to eat his prey.

THIRTY FOUR

"Well, not me. It was Bryan. He had the visitor, and then he told me," Grace said, and Valerie nodded in agreement.

Johnny smacked his head, frustrated, and then realized that his mom and Grace were teasing him. And teaching him at the same time.

Calm down and listen, he told himself.

"Okay, Bryan had a visitor. He always has visitors. What makes this one special?"

They had all met Bryan Anderson when he and his wife Rachel Winsor helped a woman who died and then returned to her past life to fix a mistake she had made. Since then, Bryan had helped many other people stuck, or waiting in the in-between, to move on.

"Well, this visitor was not someone in the in-between," Grace said.

"Okay, so they are alive now? What in the world are you two not telling me?" Johnny said, trying to keep calm and listen.

"Well," Grace said. "Yes, and no. I mean, he is alive, but he's not from around here."

Johnny refused the temptation to ask the next question. He knew Grace was enjoying giving him a hard time, but she would eventually have to tell the complete story., So he leaned back in his chair and took a bite of scone and a sip of coffee.

Grace sighed, and then laughed. "Okay, teasing over. He is not from around here, meaning he doesn't live here."

"Where does he live? Why are you being so mysterious? And he's not from the in-between. Is he from another dimension?"

"Kinda. If I understand it correctly, or if Bryan understood it correctly, it's a parallel world to this one."

"Which is another dimension," Johnny said.

"Okay. Let's say that it is."

"It is."

Valerie laughed and put her hand on her son's arm.

"Probably not the important part at the moment."

"You're right. Okay, what did this person want from Bryan?"

"Help."

"Good grief, is it possible to get more information and what this has to do with me or us?"

"I thought it would be better if Bryan told the story. He's on his way."

This time it was Johnny who laughed. "Well, I hope you two enjoyed stringing me along this way."

"Oh, we did," Grace and Valerie said together, clinking their coffee cups.

• • • ● • ● • ● • ● • •

Finding Bryan had been easy. The trees in the little park had told him where he would be. It had taken Pax a few days to understand what they were saying. The park was full of open spaces, with only small clumps of trees scattered around it. The trees had done their best to connect with each other and provide for the rest of the park. But too few trees, too much grass, and the concrete made it difficult.

Pax was used to the underground root system that spread across his world. The trees were the primary fabric of the earth, and mushrooms and other plants connected underground and above ground.

The destruction of that network in this world was what had been the most disorienting for him. The world was noisy, but it wasn't just that noise that drowned out the voices of the trees and plants. It was what they had to fight through to be heard.

One day he climbed the highest tree he could find. It was still small compared to the tree he lived in in his world, where he was often above the clouds. But as he sat in the tree's top watching the children play in the park, the traffic stopping and starting, the people rushing by, he finally heard the trees whisper like a thread running through his veins. He had often thought that hearing the trees speak was like the sap rising, and that was how he heard it that day.

He had stayed all day in the tree, knowing that Koda and Ceya would wonder where he was. But he had been so happy to hear what the tree had to say, and the tree had been so delighted to have someone listen, he couldn't bring himself to come down.

That was how he had learned about the man called Bryan. A man in Doveland, the place Isira had told him to go, who listened to the trees too. So Pax had done what Akotas had taught him. He imagined himself to Bryan's woods. Once there, he stood in the pathway where he knew Bryan would walk, and waited.

When Pax saw Bryan coming toward him, he couldn't stop smiling. It felt as if he was meeting someone he had known his whole life. He smiled at the rabbit, who hopped in front of

Bryan, leading the way. The rabbit had stopped at Pax's feet, nose twitching, and Pax had leaned over and petted him.

Bryan watched, thinking he was seeing someone from the in-between, and said, "Ah, the rabbit sees you. That's different."

Pax had smiled at Bryan and said, "I'm not what you think. Shall we follow your friend? I have a favor to ask of you."

Bryan, who had become much more used to seeing unusual people in unusual places, agreed immediately. But when he learned why Pax had come to him, he found it hard to believe.

They walked together and enjoyed the beauty of the spring day. Talking first of the joy of the woods and then of what Pax had come to ask. Bryan had said yes, and the two of them had hugged. Bryan almost cried when Pax had explained his world. It sounded like heaven to him.

After Pax left, Bryan had gone to Grace and told her, knowing she would put into motion whatever needed to be done to prepare for Pax and his friend's arrival.

And Pax had returned to the shack to find Ceya and Koda and Maya waiting for him. He didn't tell them about Bryan then. It wasn't the time. But now that Ginny had missed their meeting, he knew what he had to do.

And Johnny, after hearing Pax's story, knew what they needed to do too. Part of him was excited. It was another adventure. The other part was worried. What if they failed? It could mean the destruction of an entire world.

THIRTY FIVE

Ginny felt as if her heart would flutter out of her chest, and she could barely breathe. Was she having a panic attack?

Calm down, she told herself. Because no matter what was happening, she could not let Fred see the terror she was feeling. Unclenching her hands, she breathed in as deeply as she could, exhaled slowly, held her breath, breathed in again, repeating it until the flutter had stopped and her fear had ebbed down to where she felt in control again.

That Fred had let her hear the conversation with the man he said was his boss might have soothed her if she still believed that Fred was who he said he was. But she didn't. And that she had fallen for his pack of lies was almost more upsetting than where she found herself now. Almost.

Ginny wanted to keep calling herself a fool, but she knew it wouldn't help her. After this was all over, she would allow herself to wallow in her stupidity if that was what she wanted, but not now. If not for her, for her mother. Because what had caused the terror was hearing the voice on the other end asking about Maya, and Fred said it was under control. What was under control? How was this about her mother?

She had thought that Fred taking her was just about him and her. He wanted her for something. Something terrible probably, but it was just about her, and she was determined to escape and make her way home.

But Fred let her know it was more than that when he deliberately allowed her to hear the conversation. He wanted her to know, but why? Why would someone target her and her mother?

After that conversation, Fred had laughed, and taking his eyes off the road for a moment, he had looked at her and said, "We can probably stop with the daughter talk."

"There is no daughter, is there?"

"No, daughter. No parents. No need for a school."

She had felt her last hope drain away at that moment. That tiny bit of hoping that she had misread the situation, and he was talking to that man about a different Maya, and her seat belt really was just stuck.

He smiled, a genuine smile, pleased with himself, and looked back at the road.

"And now that you know that this is about your mother too, don't bother trying to escape because that will only make it worse for her."

Ginny didn't know if that was true. But what if it was? So she sat quietly, controlling her terror. Finally, she asked what Fred had been waiting for her to ask all along.

"What is this about, then? Why me? Why my mother? What is it you and that guy on the phone want?"

"I'm going to tell you, Ginny, but since you probably won't believe me, let's wait until we get someplace safe."

"Safe for whom?"

Fred laughed. "Whom. You said 'whom.' Most people would have said, 'safe for who.' But not you, Ginny. You pay attention to details. How did you miss that I was lying? Or the bigger picture of your life? How did you miss that your mother has lied to you your entire life? Why didn't you force her to tell you what was actually going on with your lives?

"Why not, Ginny? Is it because you are exactly what you have been telling yourself. That you are stupid and an idiot? That you were too afraid to ask for the truth?

"Only you know the answer to that. But what I know is, if you had, then you might not be in this situation. You might have had a chance. But as it stands now, you don't.

"So my suggestion to you is to lean back, close your eyes, get some sleep, because you might not get much of it once we get where we are going. Because, Ginny, I need answers and I am not afraid of asking the questions and doing what I need to do to get them."

When Ginny said nothing, Fred glanced over at her and wondered what she was thinking. She had shut herself off to him.

That's not a good thing, he thought. *I wonder if I should have approached this differently. No matter, I'll find the answer, eventually. How long it takes is entirely up to her.*

For Ginny, Fred's words had opened a door that she had kept shut her entire life. She had woken up, and she wouldn't go to sleep again. She wanted answers, too. And just like Fred, she was going to get them.

Never again would she play by rules that she knew weren't right, someone else's rules because they said so. Never again would she agree to something she knew wasn't true. She would trust herself and not believe what someone tried to convince her was true. She would stop separating herself from people, turning her thought inward on herself. And most of all, she would never agree not to do something she knew she could do.

She was awake. And she would stay that way. But she wouldn't let Fred know that. She had to continue to act as if she was under his spell, under the world's spell, even under the illusion that her mother had spun for her. Perhaps her mother had meant well and was trying to protect her, but by not letting her know the truth about something—she didn't know what yet—look where it had gotten them both.

Her mother lonely, old, miserable, and she, Ginny, had been following in her footsteps. No, she was over and done with this. All her life, she had felt as if she had a calling and ignored it. She did her best to feel fulfilled teaching, even though she knew it wasn't enough.

Yes, she loved teaching. She loved the kids, helping them become themselves, but she hadn't helped herself first. She hadn't become herself, whoever that was. Ginny would stop allowing herself to feel unwanted.

Yes, Ginny thought again. *I have woken up, and I will stay awake for myself and my mother, even if that only means staying alive until someone comes to help.*

Who that would be, Ginny hadn't a clue. But then, she hadn't a clue about anything up to now.

So she had to hope that her mother would get help because the one thing she knew about her mother is that she would never believe a story that Ginny just didn't call. Her mother would know something was wrong, and she would move heaven and hell to find her. That she knew about her mother, and what else there was to know she'd find out later. She just had to stay alive until help arrived.

And Ginny knew how to play the victim. *I've practiced it long enough,* Ginny said to herself.

So she let none of her newly found resolve show in her manner or her voice. Instead, she slunk down in her seat, and closing her eyes, said in a weak voice, "What are you going to do with me? What have I done to you?"

Fred didn't bother answering. She'd find out soon enough.

THIRTY SIX

G inny was right. Her mother was ready to move heaven and hell to find her daughter. She wanted to do something, anything. Whatever was going on was happening because of who they were. It wasn't random. She had to find Ginny and tell her the truth.

The knowledge that she had waited too long to tell her, and now it might be too late, was tearing her apart. Having nowhere to vent her feelings, she was sobbing so hard she couldn't breathe, barely registering that the boy Pax had his arms around her and was whispering that everything was going to be alright.

How could it be alright? Ever? Maya felt the familiar black cloud of despair heading her way. If she let it, it would take over, and she would be useless.

"It's okay," Pax said, and she experienced a wave of warmth, and the black cloud scuttled away.

"Let's go," Koda said, reaching for Maya, and between them, they helped her walk away from the coffee shop, Ceya staying behind to scan the crowd.

Was there anyone watching they needed to worry about? Seeing and feeling nothing other than curiosity about a woman sobbing,

Ceya sent out another wave of warmth, this one to everyone in the shop, so that they all sighed and turned away, feeling as if everything was fine and the world was a wonderful place.

And because she was cautious by nature, Ceya also sent out a frequency that made everyone's cell phone delete everything that had happened in the past fifteen minutes. Most of them would never know. Only the few that had taken a picture and videos moments before would wonder why they weren't on their phone anymore. But no one would ever connect it with what they just witnessed, because they had already forgotten about it.

Both Pax and Koda looked back at her and smiled, knowing what she had done. From now on, they needed to be even more vigilant. Someone had made their first move, and all of them knew who that person was. Dradon might not possess the same skills they did, but he had people who did what he told them to do.

For Dradon, everything was for his personal gain. His version of a better world was the one where he was in control. So Ceya's destructive wave of energy included all cameras that might have seen them. Ones Dradon would have trained on them. Perhaps he didn't know exactly where they were at that moment, but he had known where Ginny had been all along and had finally chosen to do something.

So when they reached the shack, all of them agreed when Pax said, "It's time to go."

Maya wanted to say no. She was afraid that if they left Ginny would never find them. But like her daughter, Maya decided to stop pretending everything would be okay if only she followed Dradon's rules. She had fooled herself long enough.

Instead, she said, "We need to stop at the house. There is something I can't leave behind."

"How important is it?" Koda asked.

"It's something Akotas gave me in case I ever wanted to go back to Crann. Dradon cannot find it. I'll drive back to the house as if it is a regular day, get it, and we can leave from there. I'll act like I am running off to the store to get something."

"What if Dradon is waiting for you?" Ceya asked.

"I don't think he will come for me. It's always been Ginny he has wanted. I was just the person keeping her safe until he needed her."

"For what?" Pax asked. "Why doesn't he just leave the two of you in this world and go back to Crann on his own?"

"That's the thing," Koda said. "He can't. He doesn't know how to return."

"Do you?" Pax asked.

Ceya and Koda looked at each other and sighed. But it was Maya who answered.

"They do, but they can't because we're here. Their mission is to protect us. They won't abandon us, and we can't go back without what's at the house, and I won't go back without Ginny. Isira and Akotas also knew how to travel between worlds, but they hid that secret from Dradon."

"You mean I am stuck here with you?" Pax hissed. "Ceya, did you know?"

"I did."

"And you came anyway?"

When she didn't answer, Pax forced himself to not walk away. How could Ceya have done this? How could she have come, knowing she might have to stay? *But then she would be with Koda*, Pax thought. He would have no one. He might never get to leave this hateful version of the world.

"Why didn't Isira tell me?" he whispered.

"She told you. You didn't listen. She and Akotas told you that you have a mission and that your future depends on your coming here.

"If you complete this mission, then all of us can return to Crann. I didn't know how that would happen. But Isira said it, so it has to be true," Ceya answered.

"Do you believe I can do this?"

"I wouldn't have come otherwise," Ceya said, and then looking at Koda added, "Well, perhaps I would have."

This time it was Maya who comforted Pax.

"All of us can do this together, Pax. The four of us can do this. You don't need to convince me to return to Crann if that is part of your mission. I should have never come back here. All we have to do is to get what Akotas left me, find Ginny, and we can leave here."

"As lovely and ridiculously simple as that sounds, Maya," Koda said, "we are leaving out one key element. We can't just rescue Ginny and leave. It's much more complicated. We can't leave Dradon here to continue to harm this world. So we'll have to take him with us or stop him here. Do any of you have any idea how to do that?"

Pax realized there was no use in wishing away the problem or wondering why he was the one entrusted with the mission. It was time to do what he had come to do.

"We can't do it alone. We need help. And that's why we have to get to that town called Doveland. They can help, and they're waiting." Pax said.

When Maya, Koda, and Ceya started to ask how they could be waiting, Pax held up his hand.

"Later. Let's get what Maya needs from the house and get going."

"But Ginny!" Maya wailed, despite her determination not to fall into despair and already knowing the answer. "We can't leave her."

"We're not," Pax said. "I promise."

And at that moment in time, Pax believed what he said. They would find her daughter. But he had to admit to himself that what was driving him to find Ginny was not only that she was in trouble, but that they needed to rescue her before he could go home.

He needed to get home. He couldn't live here in the noise and concrete. So no matter what it took, he would return to Crann. But first, they would get whatever Akotas gave Maya.

Secrets, he mumbled to himself. *Why did everyone keep so many secrets? Couldn't Akotas have told me what I am supposed to do and how to do it?*

Then he heard again what Ceya had said, "Isira told you, Pax, you just didn't listen."

Maybe Akotas had told him, too, and he didn't listen. Or perhaps at the time, he hadn't understood what Akotas meant.

"Let's go," Koda said.

They agreed that Koda and Ceya would fly, and Pax would hide in the back of Maya's car until they were out of town. Pax wasn't ready to tell them he could get there another way. Not yet. Yes, he was keeping secrets, too.

Was it a wise thing to do? He didn't know. But it was what he would do, anyway.

THIRTY SEVEN

After telling Johnny, Valerie, and Grace about Pax, Bryan returned to his woods. On the way, he saw a few in-betweeners, but none of them were looking for help from him, so he let them be.

Rachel and Hank were meeting about a renovation of a home she wanted to sell to a young couple moving to town. The original owners died a few years ago without leaving the house to anyone, so when the house went up for sale at an auction, she and Hank had gone in together and bought it.

It was the first time Hank and Rachel had worked together, but it was going well so far, and Bryan was happy that Rachel was doing something that gave her so much joy. Even though he understood being in the woods was where he needed to be when not helping others, he had at first felt guilty about it until Rachel assured him enough times that it was not only okay, it was necessary. For both of them. They both needed him to spend time with the trees.

Some days they took time off together and found trails within an hour or two from Doveland, and that became one of their favorite things to do together.

But right now, Bryan was waiting for Pax and his friends, and being in the woods was the best way he knew how to wait. He settled into a space just off the trail. It was in the middle of a circle of trees, surrounded by thick underbrush. He often thought of it as his nest. A bed of moss wrapped a rock that was just the right size for him to sit on. Above him, the trees arched across the sky, leaving an opening where he could see clouds drifting by, but if it rained, he stayed reasonably dry.

All the birds knew him, and within minutes of his arrival, they were back to their usual antics. The chickadees knew he kept sunflower seeds for them, and as soon as he lifted his hands, filled with seeds, they descended. Feeding them kept him distracted for a few minutes.

As soon as the seeds were gone, he settled in, imagining himself to be part of the root system that lay beneath him, the lacy threads that transmitted messages from the trees and plants to each other. And, on a good day, to him, too. It was how Pax said he found Bryan, and now Bryan wanted to see if he could find Pax. However, if Pax wasn't in the woods, he couldn't reach him.

Bryan wondered what it would be like to live somewhere that the underground system was always available. It seemed impossible to him, although he knew that long ago it had been like that in this world.

An hour later, his world's way to reach everyone vibrated in his pocket. It was a number he didn't recognize, but he answered anyway. A woman said they were on their way. Were they ready for them?

Bryan stood, his heart racing. "Yes, yes, we are. When will you be here?"

"First we have to get something important from my house. If all goes well, a few hours."

She read off an address and asked if that was correct.

Bryan confirmed it was, told her to be safe, and called Grace.

"They're on their way."

· · · · ● · ● · · ·

Maya calmed herself, parked her car, and imagining herself as the person she had been just a few hours before, bent over and shuffled across the lawn, used her key to open the door, and stepped into the house. She had kept the house alive all these years for Ginny. But now that Ginny wasn't there, she no longer cared. Would the house die without them or become something else? She didn't know, and she couldn't summon enough energy to care, either.

For a long moment, her feet stayed glued to the floor. She was afraid to move. She wanted to call out for Ginny, hoping she would answer. But she had never called out for Ginny before. Why now, when she knew she wasn't there?

The guilt felt like a hundred-pound weight sitting on her chest, making it hard to breathe. It wasn't only that Ginny was missing, but that to get what she needed, she would have to step in front of the mirror.

And although Akotas had told her that what she would see was a hologram from long ago, she was never entirely sure if that were true. As the years went by, it appeared he had aged. How could that be true if it was an old hologram? What if she had been looking into his world? What if he was watching her this way for all these years?

It had been a long time since she had looked in the mirror, passing it every morning without a glance in its direction. Even if Akotas wasn't looking, she hated to see herself fading into nothing. Useless, old, and ugly.

She prayed Akotas really couldn't see her. What would he think? Would he know she had done it to protect Ginny? That she has sacrificed the bright light that Akotas had loved about her so she didn't attract attention?

Did he know she had made a terrible mistake? Would he ever have forgiven her for it?

As she shuffled forward, hands shaking, she prepared herself to see the truth of what she had become, and if Akotas was watching his disappointment in her. Imagined or not, it would be real to her.

Allowing her focus to open to include the entire hallway, she stared into the crack, waiting for Akotas to appear. Nothing happened. She tried again. Relaxing, not looking, but looking at the same time. Still nothing. Akotas was not there anymore.

It was only her awareness of Ginny's need that kept her standing. All she wanted to do was crumble to the floor and give up. But as always, it was Ginny that pulled her back from the brink. She held onto the mirror with both hands, her forehead resting on the now-empty crack, and ran her right hand along under the frame until she found the tiny bump. She pushed. Still not looking, she felt a piece of the frame slide aside. She reached inside and took out what Akotas had given her.

"Use this, my love, when you want to return," he had said. Maya didn't know why she hadn't. She didn't even ask him how to use it, because she never intended to return to Crann. She thought she was buying freedom for Ginny by staying. She had been so wrong.

"I'm sorry," she whispered, hoping that somehow she would make up for being so selfish and stupid.

What she didn't see was Pax watching her, using the gift he hated to use. He had followed her inside the house and watched what she had done. What was in the mirror?

As Maya turned to go, Pax stepped in front of the mirror and saw himself. A small man who looked nothing like his people. A light flashed inside one of the cracks, and for a moment, he thought he saw Akotas, who waved at him.

But Maya had opened the door and was ready to leave, so he had no time to wonder at what he saw. Following her to the car, he slipped in as she opened the car door and hid behind the seat, making himself visible once again.

"Are you ready?" Maya asked, looking back at him.

Pax nodded. And then, making himself as comfortable as possible, he let himself wonder at what he had seen. Was it an illusion? A hologram? Or real?

He knew what he wanted it to be. That did not make it true, though.

THIRTY EIGHT

When Bryan called, Grace was in her apartment above her shop taking muffins out of the oven, so the timing was perfect. Since she always washed up as she baked, she was ready to go.

Grace experienced a twinge of guilt about being so pleased that someone needed their help. After all, they only needed help because they were in trouble, and she didn't want people to be in trouble. But she loved meeting new people, and the fact that she didn't have to leave Doveland to meet them, made it the perfect scenario. She didn't have to travel, but she still had adventures.

Still, there was always the worry that this time they couldn't help. Or that they would lose someone in the process. But she couldn't deny that she was excited because this adventure involved a portal and another world.

How many people would believe that story, she laughed to herself. Not many. They'd think she had lost her marbles. If she had told her friends from before Doveland, they wouldn't have believed her. They accepted the world for what they could see, and what people they trusted told them. For a time in her life, Grace thought that way, too.

No, if she was going to be honest with herself, she hadn't believed what her past friends believed. She had only pretended she did because it made being with people easier.

But then she met Suzanne, and everything changed. She met Suzanne when Suzanne lived in what she called the Earth dimension. Suzanne was from another dimension called Erda. Suzanne called the planet where both dimensions resided Gaia. It sounded crazy in her head when she thought about it, but Grace knew it was real. Before he passed on, her husband Eric had gone to live in Erda with Suzanne and their friends Sarah, Leif, and Ava's daughter Hannah.

Eric had come back to her instead of staying, knowing he wouldn't live long, but said it was worth it to spend his last days in this lifetime with her. They'd see each other again in another one.

Shaking her head as she prepared the muffins to take with her, Grace brought herself back to the present. Bryan said that Pax didn't say he was from another dimension. He called it a parallel world. That sounded like another dimension to her. Perhaps it was simply semantics.

Either way, Pax had friends who were in trouble, and Grace would get to meet them and be part of the group prepared to help and protect them. That gave her a purpose much more significant than she ever dreamed she would have in her life. Grace had all these friends who could do amazing things and help other people from other worlds. What else could she want? And although she didn't have any magical skills, she knew how to listen, provide support, and bring good things to eat.

Stopping in front of the mirror at the head of the stairs, Grace patted her hair, buttoned her sweater, and adjusted the chain on the glasses hanging around her neck.

Grace asked Hank to install a mirror because too many times she had rushed out the door, not checking what she looked like. Once,

Grace had made it halfway down the stairs before realizing she still had on her pajamas. What if she'd gone into the store that way?

The day Hank put up the mirror, he asked her if she was still okay going up and down the steps.

"Of course I am," she had huffed. And then thought about it and asked Hank to add another railing to have one on both sides and to add more lighting on the steps.

"Wise moves, old or not," she told him.

"You're not old, Grace," Hank said, leaning over and hugging her. Hugging was not Hank's typical style, so it had worried her that what he was really telling her was that she was old.

Well, she was. But not in an old and useless kind of way. Old and wise, and still lively, she had told herself that day, and she did it now. Standing in front of the mirror, she repeated an affirmation from Emile Coue she had heard many, many years before.

"Every day, in every way, I'm getting better and better."

Today, to amuse herself, she said it in French, the original way she had learned it in high school French class:

"Tous les jours à tous points de vue, je vais de mieux en mieux."

"That should do it," Grace said to herself as she made her way down the stairs, grateful for the railing on each side so that she could hold the bag of muffins in one hand and the railing with the other hand.

Valerie was waiting at the bottom of the stairs for her. Neither woman said anything as Valerie drove, heading to Ava and Evan's. They could speculate all they wanted, but it wouldn't change anything. They had to wait to hear from the people who were coming what they needed. Only then would they know how to help. They had to trust that, between all of them, someone would know what to do. But in the meantime, Ava and Evan's house was the safest place for the new arrivals. It had proven to be a safe haven for many people over the years.

Since the Anders' home was only a few miles out of town, they were there within minutes. They pulled in beside Bryan's car to the far right of the parking lot in front of the house, leaving plenty of room for the rest of the people who were coming. The part of the house facing the parking lot presented an unimposing facade. A casual visitor wouldn't notice the cameras mounted along the long driveway, the parking lot, and around the outside and inside of the house.

Inside, the house came to life. From the front door, the house spread into an open and airy space that included the living room, dining room, and kitchen that led to the back patio. From the patio, a vista spread out to the meadow, the forest beyond it, and the vegetable and flower gardens Ava kept adding to each year.

A bunkhouse stood off to the left, near the forest. A curving gravel path with flower beds on both sides led to it.

Although Ava and Evan ran a small and very private bed-and-breakfast, there were no guests at the moment. Which meant there was plenty of space to house the visitors.

Somehow it always works out that way, Grace thought. Others might believe it to be a coincidence, but she knew it wasn't.

THIRTY NINE

Once they were a few blocks away from the house, Maya pulled over, and Pax moved into the passenger seat. Maya wanted the feeling of security of having someone sitting beside her, and Pax wished to observe more of this world that he'd fallen into. So far, this world had not impressed him, even though Maya said that the town they were in was one where people liked to live.

Looking out the window at the other houses, Pax asked Maya why her home was the only one falling apart. How could she live in a place like that?

"I wanted people to be afraid of it and leave us alone," Maya said.

Pax didn't answer. This world made no sense to him. He couldn't understand how anyone would consider this jumble of enormous homes, small grass-filled yards and few trees, a nice place to live.

To his eyes, used to a diversity of shapes and sizes and the colors of the forest and meadows of his world, the box-like structures appeared ugly. Although they passed a few houses with trees, the trees looked so lonely that he had trouble looking at them.

In his world, they lived in small communities, not spread out on long streets. Sometimes they lived in long buildings made from trees or mud. sometimes in tents and sometimes in caves or underground. Everyone had their own space, but just enough. No one had bigger spaces than another to show their wealth or power. If you had something, you shared it because there was always more.

This world felt as if people were afraid all the time that they wouldn't have enough, so they had to control what they had and take more. Pax guessed they felt that way because they no longer lived with nature. They got rid of it.

In his world, they lived in and with the trees. They only used what was necessary and available. Communities shared. No one hoarded. People recognized greed as something that would destroy. It was a simple life compared to this world. He ached everywhere with the missing of it.

Sometimes they passed a house with flowers, and the riot of spring colors cheered him and then saddened him, remembering his home where the flowers grew with wild abandon. Home. He couldn't even think of the word without wanting to lean his head on the door and let himself cry. But he couldn't. There was no time.

Besides, after they left the town and headed to Doveland, there were more trees. Leaning his head on the window he could see the sky and he wondered if two of the birds he saw soaring above them were Koda and Ceya. He envied them their ability to fly above all this.

Let me count all the ways I am not good at this, Pax said to himself.

As if she heard him, Maya said the first words she had spoken since they left the house.

"Thank you, Pax. I am profoundly grateful that you're here."

Pax turned to look to see if she was mocking him. Akotas had sometimes done that to get him to snap out of his, what Akotas called, pity party moods.

But she wasn't. She was serious. Her eyes on the road, she reached over and touched his hand and once again said, "Thank you."

"For what? I have done nothing, and now Ginny is missing. There is nothing to thank me for."

"I know how hard it is for you to be here."

Pax said nothing at first. Instead, he watched as the trees flashed by. It was strange to be in a container called a car to get somewhere and to have other cars pass them or travel with them. They walked, ran, or thought themselves somewhere in his world, the underground network of roots giving directions.

Before he went home, he thought perhaps he would like to fly in one of the metal containers Ceya told him was a plane. That was something he couldn't do at home, see the world from so high in the sky. He could see from his tree, but had never seen the world like a bird.

Bringing himself back to the present, he said, "Yes, it is. But I am learning about things I would never have known before. I guess if I were born here, I would be used to it and would have missed it like you did when you came to our world."

"There's one big difference, though, Pax. I should have stayed there, and you should not stay here."

"Why did you leave?" Pax asked, as gently as he could, knowing this answer would be painful for Maya.

"I thought I missed the hustle and bustle of this world. I didn't see how I could be myself in your world. It was so community-oriented that I believed that meant I had to be like everyone else. Only after I left did I realize no one asked me to change, that I could have been myself there. But I was too young and naïve then. I loved Akotas, and I thought he loved me enough to come back with me. But he said he couldn't. He had an obligation to remain in Crann and help his people, along with his sister.

"I didn't understand that either. A bigger obligation than his personal wants and needs? That seemed so foreign to me then. Your coming here has shown me again what he meant. I know you didn't want to come, but you felt that your mission was more important than what you wanted.

"Which is why I thanked you, Pax. No matter what happens, I am grateful that you have come."

Maya flicked on her turn signal and turned into a rest stop. Once the car stopped, she turned to face Pax.

"I wanted to say this to you, and make sure you know I mean it. Pax, no matter what happens, if you need to choose between saving yourself or me, save yourself. Save Ginny. Nothing else matters."

After a long silence, while Pax looked at Maya and saw past the facade she had taken on, he said, "I understand why Akotas fell in love with you. Yes, I agree. I will save Ginny. Not only for you, but for my people. They need her to guide Crann when Isira is gone."

Maya's eyes filled with tears. "I have been afraid to ask. And you all have been kind enough not to say. But does that mean that Akotas has died?"

Pax nodded, and Maya burst into tears. Once again, Pax found himself comforting Maya. It was a strange sensation, not one he had ever experienced before, but when he forgot how he felt and thought about how she felt, it was easier.

What he didn't add was that he wasn't so sure anymore that Akotas had died. Akotas had left one day, saying it was his time. That was what everyone said as they prepared to leave one lifetime and move to the next. But did he mean that? Or did he mean it was his time to do something else?

After Maya pulled herself together and they resumed their trip, she told him about the mirror and how she would see Akotas in the crack, how Akotas told her what she saw would be a hologram. But it seemed to change, so how could that be? And today, he was no longer there.

Pax didn't tell her he thought he saw Akotas wave at him, because he didn't know what it meant. He didn't want to get her hopes up. They had enough trouble dealing with what was in front of them. First, they needed to find Ginny. Then convince her to leave this world and come to Crann. And finally, do something to contain Dradon so he stopped making this world worse, and ensure that he could never affect Crann again.

No big deal, he said to himself, hoping that it would make him feel better. It didn't.

FORTY

While all the people who wanted to help her headed to Doveland, Fred took Ginny in the opposite direction. Ginny had stopped talking, and it delighted Fred because it left him time to think. Plan. Make sure that everything was in place.

He had prepared for this moment for years. He hadn't known exactly what would happen or precisely what he would do, but he had known that someday he would find Dradon's weakness and use it against him. That Dradon's weakness was this woman made it both more delightful and more complicated.

Delightful because until he kidnapped her, Ginny had been excellent company, and he liked her. Fred didn't want to admit that he did, but he had always prided himself on being honest with himself, which made it complicated because he had to use Ginny to get what he wanted. How he would use her wasn't clear, but now that he had done this, he knew it could not be the same between the two of them ever again.

For a moment, Fred wished not only that he could fix his relationship with Ginny, but that she would then help him take over Dradon's empire. In hindsight, Fred thought that might have been the better way. He should have won her over first and then convinced her of the rightness of what he was doing. He could have explained away the fake daughter somehow.

You're fooling yourself, Fred said to himself. Ginny had stopped talking and was either sleeping or pretending to sleep. Either way, she would never forgive him for what he had done, so he would have to use whatever tools he had to keep her in line. Once he figured out why she was so crucial to Dradon and hid her and himself so Dradon couldn't find them, he'd make a deal. The girl for the kingdom. *So medieval,* Fred thought.

• • • ● • ● • ● • • •

Ginny wasn't sleeping. She was thinking and listening, hoping to get some insight into the situation. Why would Fred be kidnapping her? Why did he target her in the first place, claiming to have a daughter? And why wait until this day? It had to be to stop her from meeting her mother. The timing was too perfect for it to be anything else.

So what was he trying to keep her from knowing? It was the answer to that question that Ginny wanted. Had her mother finally decided to tell her what she had been keeping from her? Because that much she was sure of—her mother was going to tell her something important. But what?

There had never been a moment in Ginny's life when she hadn't felt as if she was different from everyone else. To make herself fit in, she got very good at adapting to circumstances and what other people wanted. She worked hard to please people by being what they expected. She made sure she was always available to be helpful. That should have made her feel good, but often it made her feel fake since she didn't want to do most of what she did, and a part of her resented she was always the one who had to conform to please others.

In the car with Fred, thinking back on her life, Ginny wanted to give up. She was tired of it all. Maybe it would all go away if she did whatever Fred wanted her to do. What that could be, Ginny couldn't imagine. Well, she could, but he had shown no signs of being a sexual predator, and although that might have been why he had taken her, she didn't think so. The more she thought about it, the more she just wanted to wallow in her misery.

But she knew she couldn't. Miserable or not, she was a fighter. She would use the skills she had to get out of this situation. She'd let Fred believe she was giving in and was doing what he wanted. She'd give him no outward sign of resistance. She'd let him see her worry for her mother, but not her fear of him. She'd practiced her chameleon abilities all her life. They would come in handy now.

So when Fred said they would have to stop for the night, she sighed and said, "Good. I'm exhausted. And hungry. Could we eat?"

She reveled in a quiet satisfaction that he seemed startled by her request. But Fred recovered quickly and asked, "Anything specific you would like?"

"Anything, really. I haven't eaten since a sandwich at lunchtime."

"Okay, we'll find a motel and then get some food."

"Sounds great," Ginny said with a grateful smile.

Fred smiled back, thinking that this was going to be more fun than he thought. She was playing him, but that was okay. He'd been playing her the whole time. It seemed fair that she would try to turn the tables on him. He'd go along with the game, but he wouldn't fall for her act.

She was much more wily than he had thought. But he was much smarter than she knew. He'd win in the end. But in the meantime, he could enjoy himself. Mind games were his favorite.

All he needed to do was keep her reasonably happy and safe. He was sure that a dead Ginny would not be of any use to Dradon. But an injured one would be okay.

For what seemed like the hundredth time, his phone vibrated in his jacket pocket. He knew it was Dradon, wanting to know what was going on. Dradon was too smart to fall for his lame reports about Ginny's safety. And he was sure Dradon had been tracking him the entire time and would know he was moving west. Dradon would be smoking hot angry by now.

Once they stopped, he'd call him back and make up a story about how he and Ginny decided to go away together for the weekend.

"Yes," he'd say, "She seems to have taken a liking to me."

Dradon would be pleased, or at least pretend to be, but at least he would calm him down for the night.

And that's what he did. While Ginny went to the restroom, he guarded the door so no one else could come in. After checking to make sure there was no window where she could escape, Fred made the phone call.

On the other end, Dradon paused and then asked why he had gotten so friendly with the girl.

"You were just supposed to watch her, not get to know her."

Smiling, Fred answered, "Yes, but it was more effective to do it this way. Now I have control and can bring her to you whenever you wish."

"I wish," Dradon shouted over the phone, "for you to bring her to me first thing tomorrow. I want to see your car heading my way."

"Of course, sir," Fred answered, making his voice the mix of simpering and calm that he had practiced for so long.

"In the morning," he said, knowing that was exactly what he would not do. In the morning, Fred's phone and the tracker on his car would go one way, but he and Ginny would go another.

FORTY ONE

At the same time Grace and Valerie pulled into the front of the house, Ceya and Koda landed in the Anders' backyard. Ava had been standing in the kitchen looking out the window, admiring the blooms on the two dogwoods they had added to the yard last autumn, when she noticed two hawks land in the yard.

How wonderful, she thought. She and Evan had become invested in providing habitat for as many birds and animals as possible on their property, so new bird sightings made her happy. She picked up a bowl of salad she made to prepare for the people coming to the house and glanced back one more time at the hawks, just in time to see them transform into a man and a woman.

Startled, she dropped the bowl, salad spilling out everywhere on the counter, and let out a little screech. Evan, who had been setting the table, turned and saw what had made Ava squeal and rushed to her.

"OMG," Ava said. "Are these our visitors? Bryan didn't tell us they would be birds!"

In the yard, Ceya turned to Koda and said, "Oops. Maybe we should have done that in the woods?"

"Too late now," he said as he waved to the man and woman in the window. "Might as well introduce ourselves."

Bryan had seen the two birds, too. He had been in the woods by the bunkhouse, waiting. Bryan thought it would be his new friend Pax who would arrive first, and hoped to walk with him in the forest before anything else happened. But once the two birds became people, he realized it wouldn't work out that way, so he stepped out of the woods and headed towards the arrivals.

Koda saw Bryan coming and stepping in front of Ceya, waited to see who he was, both of them ready to fly away if they were in danger. But Bryan was doing what he always did as he walked. He pulled in his energy so that it didn't expand out from him, scaring away his forest friends. So, within a few seconds, Koda and Ceya relaxed and waited, all three of them sizing one another up.

Koda and Ceya saw a quiet man with blond hair and blue eyes. a man who blended into his surroundings. They felt at peace with him immediately.

On the other hand, Bryan experienced a moment of jealousy as he looked at the man and the woman. Even as people, they looked like birds. It wasn't Koda's straight red hair, Ceya's soft white curly hair, or what they wore. It was the look in their eyes and the way they perched on their feet as if they would fly away at any moment.

He wished he didn't look so ordinary. He wished he could fly. Instead, he looked like millions of other people. His only gift was that he saw people in the in-between, and now people from a parallel world. And then he realized how ridiculously he was behaving. His life was filled with magic and love. He stilled the yearning, stuffing it where it wouldn't bother him, and extended his hand to introduce himself.

Koda, a long-time resident of this world, extended his hand and introduced himself and Ceya. Bryan was filled with questions, but he saw Ava and Evan, joined by Grace and Valerie, watching from the window, and he knew they would want to hear everything too.

By the time they reached the back patio, Hank and Rachel had arrived, and he rushed to embrace Rachel, overflowing with gratitude that she was now his wife. A moment later, Johnny walked around the house after taking Ben to spend the night at their home with his dad and Lex. So there was another round of introductions before Ava asked if they all wanted to eat outside. It didn't surprise her when everyone answered yes.

Within a few minutes, Evan and Hank had moved the table settings outside, and Grace and Ava brought out the food. As always, there were all kinds of food, minus the salad, but it was Bryan who asked Ceya and Koda if what they had provided was something they could eat.

Ceya looked at the table spread with a variety of offerings and smiled at everyone.

"This looks beautiful, and yes, many things."

She reached over and held Koda's hand, and the two of them touched foreheads before turning back to the table and smiling even more before Ceya added, "This is the first time since I came to this world that it feels okay to be here. Thank you."

Tears came to Grace's eyes at those words. It was how she always felt when they all got together. They belonged to each other, and that made their own world more filled with peace and love.

Bryan waited as long as he could before asking, "When will Pax be here?"

"Soon," Koda answered. "If you like, I could check on them?"

"No need," Johnny said. "They are only a few minutes away."

Koda took a long look at Johnny before saying anything.

"I understand why Isira sent us here."

"Isira?" Grace asked.

A quiet settled over the table. The moon had risen, and the stars were becoming visible in the darkening sky. It was as if the universe was pausing between day and night in the same way that they were pausing before learning what they would face together.

"We'll wait," Grace said, and everyone understood what she meant.

FORTY TWO

As Johnny had said, they didn't need to wait long. Watching the camera on the front of their house, Ava saw the car pull up and two people get out.

"Perhaps the two of you should meet them?" She suggested to Ceya and Koda.

Koda added, "Bryan, why not come, too. Pax knows you, too."

Bryan couldn't hide his smile. These people trusted him. For some reason, it fed a part of himself that he hadn't realized had been hungry.

As soon as the three of them left to meet the arrivals, Ava stopped watching the camera, thinking they might need their privacy. Instead, she set two more places and then sat with the rest of her friends, trying to remain calm but feeling a welling of both excitement and worry.

She loved making their house a sanctuary. For a moment, she flashed back to when she ran away from it, believing that Evan wouldn't love her if he knew what she had been before. It had been such a stupid thing to do, run from people that loved her, but she had let fear drive her instead of reason. Good things came out of that time, though, starting with finding her Uncle Hank. Neither realized that the other existed, but once they found each other, both of them changed. She lost her fear that she wasn't loved, and Hank learned he wasn't a wicked man after all.

She smiled across the table at Hank, and he tipped his head, smiled one of his crooked smiles back at her, and then stood as Bryan and the newcomers came around the side of the house.

Grace stepped forward to greet them, extending her hand to Pax, who, having learned the custom, shook hands and then bowed. Turning to the woman with him, Grace opened her arms, and Maya fell into them. The hug surprised no one at the table, having experienced the healing of Grace's embrace.

"Welcome," Grace said. "Come sit by me."

Pax had already moved to the seat beside Bryan and the woman Bryan introduced as his wife Rachel. It was a relief to find that he experienced a sense of peace with Bryan and Rachel.

Did Bryan realize, Pax asked himself, *how much like a bird this woman Rachel was?* Her red hair was almost the same as Koda's, and her eyes took in everything. She perched like Koda and Ceya. Pax was happy for his new friend and also faintly jealous because he believed he would never have a love like theirs in his life. He was too different from everyone else. He knew all the women in his clan. None of them were for him.

By then the sun had slipped past the horizon, so they ate under a sliver of a moon. The soft lighting that surrounded the patio gave off enough light to see, but not block out the stars. They all acted as if there was nothing unusual about people from two different worlds, two dimensions, sitting together having dinner.

While they ate, the visitors answered questions about Crann and the people who lived there, and a short version of how Akotas, Isira, and Dradon had fallen from the cliff. The more Bryan heard about Crann, the more he wanted to visit and wondered if it was possible. At one point, Pax leaned in and whispered, "If it is, we would love to have you," which made Bryan so happy he couldn't stop smiling.

After they cleared the dishes, Maya asked the question Ceya, Koda, and Pax hoped she would ask.

"Who are you, people?"

It was Ava who answered, smiling as she did.

"We are often asked that question when we meet new friends. And the answer is simple. We are people who can and want to help."

"Isira sent me here. How did she know?" Pax asked.

"I suspect she might have met some of our friends when she came here years ago. But that was before we all moved to Doveland. So how she knew we would be here to help is a mystery. But our friends knew many things, so it's possible they knew who we would become before we did."

"Are they still here? Could we ask them?"

Ava shook her head. "No, they left to go back to their world, or dimension, years ago. But not before making sure some of us met before they left."

"So you are used to the idea of alternate worlds?" Koda asked.

"We are," Johnny answered. "And we are used to helping, using any gifts we might have."

"I can't do what others here do, but I can tell when people are exhausted," Grace said. "And all of you are. Maya, we understand you need to find your daughter Ginny, but from what Bryan told us about what is going on, I believe we can assume that Ginny is safe. At least for now."

"I agree," Ava said. "Everyone is tired. Hank can take Koda, Ceya, and Pax to the bunkhouse, and Maya can stay with us in the house. Does anyone else want to stay the night?"

Valerie looked at Grace, who answered for the two of them.

"Not us. I need to check on the store, and Valerie probably wants to go home to her husband and son."

"As much as I want to talk more about your world," Bryan said, "I understand this isn't the time. Rachel and I will see you tomorrow."

What Bryan didn't say was that he had seen someone from the in-between when they went to meet Maya and Pax. A man had been standing in the parking lot. He needed to see if the man was still there and if he was asking for help.

That left Johnny.

"If you don't mind," Johnny said. "I think I'll stay here."

"Happy to have you," Evan said, clapping him on the back.

"You can stay with me," Hank said, and Johnny nodded. Hank was one reason he had not followed in his father's footsteps. Johnny loved and looked up to Hank. It would embarrass Hank if he ever said it out loud, but he tried his best to make sure that Hank knew how much he meant to him.

"That's settled then," Ava said.

Turning to Maya, she extended her hand, and when Maya took it, she experienced a ripple of hope. Perhaps it was possible to stop Dradon and find Ginny. And even someday, once again experience life as something joyful, without the weight of sadness pressing down on her.

Later, lying in bed, she imagined herself as she used to be, with Akotas beside her, their baby daughter lying between them. When regret tried to force itself into her thinking, she pushed it out. Now was not the time to feel sorry for herself.

She imagined herself turning to smile at Akotas and let herself imagine he was smiling back at her. She imagined he whispered, "All is well, my love," before falling asleep, feeling safer than she had felt for many years.

Johnny didn't immediately follow Hank, Pax, Ceya, and Koda to the bunkhouse. Instead, he sat outside under the stars and searched for a missing girl.

FORTY THREE

Fred had taken no chances. After letting Ginny get ready for bed, he handcuffed one of her arms to the bed frame, taking no pleasure in the terror he saw in her eyes as he did so. That surprised him. Not the terror in her eyes, his reaction to it.

Not only did he not get off on it, as he assumed he would given his determination to ruin Dradon, but Fred felt sick to his stomach about it.

In all the years of his imagining that he would enjoy whatever it took to make Dradon suffer, he never thought through what he might have to do to rid himself of that man. And he never imagined that it would be a woman that held the key to his power grab. A kind, beautiful woman too, who, as far as he could tell, had done nothing to deserve this kind of treatment.

But he let none of that show. Instead, he kept the frozen face, the emotionless one he practiced all these years, and assured Ginny he wasn't interested in her. He needed to keep her for someone else.

Which, of course, produced more terror, which made him turn away and then slam the bathroom door, shocking himself even more. He never lost his temper. He learned to control it years before, so Dradon would accept him within his private circle.

No one suspected he was plotting to take over. He was a quiet but capable servant.

That he knew he wasn't a quiet servant didn't excuse the door slamming. But he was furious. Furious with himself for feeling something for Ginny. And furious about the situation. He needed to think clearly. Emotions were not part of his plan, nor his life.

That's what he told himself as he lay in the other bed, very aware of Ginny's breathing, trying to plan out the logical way to destroy Dradon and use Ginny without hurting her. But nothing he came up with worked. Every scenario involved turning her over to Dradon in exchange for his takeover of Dradon's empire.

It wasn't just Ginny that would enable this to happen. He had the votes. He had accumulated enough information on each one of the board members to force them to vote for him. Dradon would get Ginny for whatever he was going to use her for, and he would get the power he worked for all his life.

So even though he couldn't seem to let go of worrying about Ginny's future, he could not let it stop him from accomplishing his dream. Although he didn't know what Dradon wanted with Ginny, he knew Dradon never stopped destroying people to get what he wanted. If he needed to eliminate Ginny, Dradon would not hesitate.

Lying awake, Fred thought through his plan. He had a place to take Ginny, which would give him time to bargain for what he wanted. And perhaps, in the end, he might save her. But it couldn't, and wouldn't, be his primary objective. He had planned too long for this, and a woman, even this one, would not stop him.

• • • • ● • ● • ● • • •

Fred was right. Dradon was furious. That girl held the secret to how he could return to Crann. He was sure of it. But not the girl herself. She knew nothing. It was her mother who knew the secret. He knew Maya would never reveal it to him. She'd die first.

He had left her alone all these years because he hadn't been ready to return to Crann before. Now he was. It was time to force Maya into compliance. Ginny was the way to accomplish this. Then he would take care of them both. He could never let Ginny get to Crann and take her position as a High Priestess.

But Dradon recognized that Fred was betraying him. He suspected Fred planned to use Ginny to get what he wanted. Dradon had long suspected that Fred was not the milk-toast man that he pretended to be. However, Fred was useful, so he kept him around.

After years of Fred's compliance, Dradon had let his defenses down. Now he realized he'd been a fool to assign Fred to watch over Ginny. He made a mistake. But he could and would fix it.

Fred thought he was in control. He wasn't. For now, Dradon would let Fred keep the girl because Maya would believe that Dradon was the one who took her. It would be easy to convince Maya to help him return to Crann if he promised her Ginny would be safe. Not a promise he would keep. But Maya wouldn't risk her daughter's life.

However, before he did anything, he needed a good night's sleep. He had nothing to worry about. Maya had caved to his demands for all these years. She would cave in again. That it was Fred, not him, who had Ginny was only a minor snag in his plan.

Before falling asleep, Dradon stared at himself in the mirrored ceiling. It was his habit to talk to himself every night and every morning, to remind himself that he was a god in this world and he would be a god in the other world once he returned because the people of both worlds were too stupid to figure out how to stop him.

Dradon observed himself lying in his bed, his brown hair now gone gray, almost the color of his eyes. Yes, he was older and heavier than he had been when he fell off that cliff, but he was also more capable. He was young and reckless then, yet he still convinced people to revolt against the peace they were experiencing. This world honed his skills as he watched many of the world leaders convince people to do something that would only harm them in the end.

The ability to change worlds and make them better for himself turned him on. Yes, he learned from the influential leaders of this world, and now he was ready to become the one ruler of Crann. He would keep his power here, but he would be the only power there.

But first, he needed to get the secret of how to move back and forth between worlds.

"I'm coming for you, Maya," he said into the mirror.

Then smiling at himself, he rolled over and fell asleep, sure that all was well for him and would only get better from here on. No more playing nice guy with Maya. His time had come, and Maya and Ginny's was ending.

FORTY FOUR

Inside Hank's room, Pax lay awake, staring at the ceiling. On the one hand, he marveled at the softness of the sheets and blankets on his bed. Yet, he hated every minute of lying there.

As pleasant as the bunkhouse was, he felt extremely uncomfortable. All he could think about was getting outside into the trees that he could hear calling to him. He waited until he assumed Hank was asleep and then moved to slip out.

As he reached the door, Hank said, "There's a sleeping bag by the door. Use that."

Although he couldn't see Hank in the dark, he could see the shape in the other bed.

"Thank you," he whispered.

As he made his way out to the trees that grew near the bunkhouse, he thought that he might have misjudged the people of this world—at least some of them.

Inside the bunkhouse, Hank turned over, hoping he could now get to sleep. But his nature was to watch for danger. Perhaps it was because of his violent father and then the men he had worked for, or maybe he was born that way. Sometimes it annoyed him. Other times, he was grateful.

This was one of those times he was both grateful and annoyed. Annoyed, because he really wanted to go to sleep, and was grateful he could help someone so far from home.

Hank was also thankful to Bryan for suggesting the sleeping bag. Bryan had explained that Pax lived in trees in his world, and he might not be comfortable in the bunkhouse. Pax had lasted less than an hour. Finally, after trying every position possible in his bed, Hank fell into an uneasy sleep.

Outside, Pax put the sleeping bag under a massive oak, sighed, said goodnight to the forest, and fell asleep feeling the beat of the forest's communication that stretched out beneath him, and the safety these strangers had provided for him and his fellow travelers.

Ceya and Koda heard Pax head outside, giggled over a bet they made about how long he would last in the bunkhouse, and wondered if they should follow him. But the joy of lying together in a bed kept them still. Ceya fell asleep first, her head on Koda's shoulder. Koda tipped his head to hers, sighed with happiness at having her near him again, and slipped off to the same uneasy sleep as Hank's.

In the house, Maya had barely gotten under the covers before she fell asleep. The exhaustion of keeping up appearances had finally overtaken her and feeling safe, she let go.

Johnny, not having any luck finding Maya's daughter, drove home instead of staying with Hank. His mother, Craig, Lex, and Ben, were already asleep when he got there. He fell into bed, clothes still on, still searching for Maya's daughter, when he too fell asleep.

Bryan had stopped outside of the house and looked for the man he had seen earlier. Rachel sat in the car waiting for him, a blanket wrapped around her. She didn't want to turn on the car and keep the people in the house awake, but the air was getting colder. May was like that. It could be summer one moment and turn cold the next. She was a little worried about the plants she had started growing and decided that once they got home, she would cover them. A frost alert had popped up on her phone, and she had learned to take those alerts seriously.

She always started her plants too early. Every spring she told herself to wait, but the joy of watching green things sprout was something she could never put off after a long winter. Besides, it wasn't hard to cover them during the few touches of frost they would have. She enjoyed taking care of things, plants, houses, and people that she loved. Especially Bryan. She loved taking care of him, as he took care of her in his own way. After all these years, they had finally come together, and she couldn't be happier.

Now she watched him in the dark, looking for someone he assumed needed his help, but he wasn't sure. He told Rachel that when they first arrived he had a fleeting glimpse of a tall man leaning against the beech tree beside the parking lot. Rachel, of course, hadn't seen him. She only saw people in the in-between if she had her hand on Bryan, and only if they had come to him for help.

Bryan saw them all. But thankfully, not all of them wanted his help. The in-between was where some people went to after they passed through the door called death. Not everyone. Most people immediately moved into life on the other side.

But some people didn't realize they'd died, or they felt as if they had to stay, or they couldn't find their way out. It was the people who wanted to leave but couldn't find their way out that Bryan helped. She helped, too, keeping Bryan grounded in this lifetime.

After an hour of waiting and shivering, she whispered to Bryan, "Come on, honey, he'll find you if he needs you."

Bryan pushed himself off the house wall, stepped carefully through the garden that Ava tended, and slid into the driver's seat. It wasn't until they pulled out of the driveway, the heater blasting in the car, that Bryan finally spoke.

"I don't know if the man I saw was from the in-between."

"You mean it might have been a 'real' person?"

"No. That couldn't be. Otherwise, the cameras would have seen him."

"Well, who do you think you saw? Because you saw someone, didn't you?"

"I did."

Bryan waited until he pulled into their garage before he said anything else. Rachel, used to Bryan thinking before he spoke, and knowing he eventually would tell her, waited.

"Yes, I saw someone. I'm sure of that."

"So he wasn't dead. And he wasn't alive. What was he?"

"From another world?" Bryan said.

Rachel shucked off the blanket and got out of the car.

"Okay. But he wasn't there, so he doesn't need you now. Sleep is calling me. He'll get back to you if he needs you."

Bryan took Rachel's hand and pulled her in close, kissing her freckled nose, and smoothing back the strands of dark red hair that had escaped from her ponytail, said, "You know I love you, don't you?"

Rachel smiled and said, "Yes, And I love you even more."

FORTY FIVE

Isira stood on the edge of the cliff and watched the sunrise as she did every day. Even though it was foolish, she kept hoping that she would see the travelers return and everything would be fine. But they didn't. And every day of hoping drained her bit by bit. She was tired, and afraid, and lonely.

She couldn't remember the last time she felt happy. Actually, she could, but it was so long ago it was as if she was remembering someone else's life. In that barely remembered life, she had spent her childhood learning how to be a kind, loving, and effective leader like her parents.

She and Akotas and Dradon were not only siblings, they had been friends. They played the same as all the other children of the village. But at home, they had the extra responsibilities of learning how to be the guardians of Crann's peace.

All three readily accepted the mantel that passed down to them after William Sky chose their family. It was an honor that they cherished, and she and her brothers were bound together in that honor. She had been happy. They had all been happy.

And then, almost overnight, things changed. Although Dradon had always been different and sometimes difficult, one day he stopped trying to be good. Or stopped caring that he wasn't. Or maybe one day they all noticed what he had been all along. He wanted to be the best leader Crann had ever known, in his own way. He wanted to rule everyone and everything. That made him feel good, he said. The more their parents tried to point him back to what they expected of him, the more he resisted.

At first, they all thought it was a phase he was going through. She and Akotas would do everything they could to bring him back into their playful games. But nothing worked. It was as if the Dradon they thought he was had died and was replaced by a different Dradon. And it was that Dradon they banished.

Looking back, Isira realized Dradon had always been the boy who had to win at all costs, but they all had turned a blind eye to the problem until they couldn't anymore.

But Dradon not only survived, he also found more strength. He convinced people to follow him and taught them to be warriors. Not peaceful warriors. Fighters. He searched for, found, and fed the kernel of discontent they felt and grew it into full-blown anger. And then Dradon directed their anger into waging war.

Their parents couldn't accept what was happening. They understood how to govern within a peaceful land, but not in a war. And that it was their son causing the war broke their hearts. Akotas and Isira watched as their parents slowly gave up, and that giving up eventually killed them.

Still, Isira and Akotas held to the hope that Dradon would come to his senses. Even that day on the cliff, they had hoped Dradon had changed, and the three of them would guide a peaceful Crann together.

How foolish we were, Isira mused. She thought back to the fight and the push and her decision to go after them. Now she understood that Dradon's fall off the cliff and his refusal to come home probably saved Crann from destruction. Without Dradon fanning the flames of discontent, she had stopped the fighting.

And then Akotas returned with his wife and it seemed as if their family would go on and peace would remain the way of life in Crann.

But Maya wasn't happy. She missed the bustle of the world she came from, and she wanted their daughter to experience it. Isira knew Maya had believed that Akotas would go with her, but he stayed to fulfill his duty to their world.

Nothing he or she said convinced Maya to stay, so Akotas let her go, hoping she would return to him of her own choice. He gave her a way to come back to him. And yet, she hadn't. And then Akotas had stepped away and left the guidance of Crann to her.

Yes, she was lonely. And now she was so tired she didn't know how to continue. She had no one to talk to, no one to stand beside her as she did her best every day for her people while worrying about what would happen when she was gone.

She missed Ceya, the only person she could talk to who understood how she felt since Akotas had gone. But sending Ceya and Pax to the other world to get Maya and Ginny seemed like the only solution. It was a dangerous decision for her to make. If the two of them failed to find Maya and Ginny and bring them back to Crann, there would be no one to guide the people of her world. And she needed time with Ginny to teach her what she needed to know. Time that Isira knew in her heart was in short supply for her.

And they had to bring Dradon with them. And once he was back, they had to find a way to contain him. And Isira didn't know if they could. They were playing with fire, without a solution to putting it out.

Isira had stood so long at the cliff pondering her problems that she hadn't noticed that the sun had risen, turning the sky a fiery red, and dark clouds were forming in the north. The hairs on her arms rose as she felt the sudden temperature drop. She knew spring storms could be dangerous, with strong winds and sometimes hail that could cut through clothes and skin like a knife.

A sudden gust of wind caught her hair, now streaked with gray, and blew it across her face so hard it caused the tears that had gathered in her eyes to overflow. She wiped them away. She had no time for tears.

A crash in the forest shook the ground, and Isira stumbled. She recognized that sound. The wind had caught a dead tree and dropped it. These storms were dangerous, but they also spread seeds and pollen and cleared trees to make room for new growth. It just depended on how safe you were while it was happening. And in the open was not safe.

Isira turned, her clothes whipping around her, and walked as quickly as she could back to the village. She knew her people were preparing to weather the storm, knowing what to do passed down from generation to generation. Perhaps she just needed to have a bit more faith in what Pax was doing. A fleeting hope passed through her. She just needed to hold out a little longer and remind herself that sometimes storms can be a good thing.

Another swirl of wind almost knocked her off her feet, taking some of that hope away.

And sometimes, winds destroy, Isira said to herself.

FORTY SIX

It was Ava and Evan who first saw the coming storm. Evan had kept his promise to Ava that he would always bring Ava her first cup of coffee in the morning. He always meant to get it to her while she was still in bed. But Ava was often up long before the sun rose and was usually outside before he could get the coffee to her.

She told him it was the same. It wasn't the bed part that counted. It was that he brought coffee and himself to her each morning. That was keeping his promise.

Saturday morning wasn't any different. The two of them were outside on the back patio watching the sun rise into a dark red sky when the wind picked up, and the town's tornado warning siren sounded. Although located at the fire station in town, it could be heard far out into the countryside. Everyone understood what it meant. Find cover.

Although tornado warnings were something new to both of them when they moved to Pennsylvania, Ava and Evan were now used to it happening at least a few times each year. Well, mostly used to it. Because, as Ava said, it always struck a moment of terror.

Where she grew up, they had earthquakes and fires, and she thought she had escaped the panic that both of them brought. The first time she heard the tornado siren, she had stood hands over her ears, paralyzed, not knowing what it meant or what to do. Now, they both recognized what it meant and what to do—get to safety.

Usually, nothing came of the warnings. But it was foolish to ignore them. It had been many, many years since a tornado came close to the town of Doveland, but preparation was always wise, and they built a fully prepared basement for times like this, just in case.

But first, they needed to round everyone up and get them there. They knew Hank would take care of the people in the bunkhouse, which had a basement, too, but he would bring them to the main one since there was time.

The siren woke Maya, and she was already dressed by the time Ava knocked on her door. Within a few minutes, everyone made it down the stairs, including Pax, who, although he had never heard a siren before, knew what the trees told him and was already inside the bunkhouse door by the time Hank had gotten Koda and Ceya to follow him.

Inside the cellar, coffee was brewing. Evan had brought the food they had prepared for breakfast down with him, and when the lights went out, the built-in generator kicked on. Watching the outside cameras, they could see the wind bending the trees and sending branches flying through the air, but they were safe and warm inside.

"We have underground places like this in our world," Ceya said.

"Not as cozy as this one," Koda said, and Pax nodded, thinking how strange it was to feel comfortable and safe with people who came from another world.

Ava and Evan were thinking the same thing. And now that they had nowhere else to go, and it was doubtful anyone would be outside in this storm, inside this safe place was the perfect time to hear the story of why Koda, Ceya, Maya, and Pax had come to them.

"It's time," Ava said, and everyone understood what she meant. Since the rest of the circle was inside their own safe place, she called them on the computer so that they could hear the story too. Rachel and Bryan huddled together under a blanket in their basement, and Ava made a note to upgrade their basement for them once this was over.

Grace had gone to Valerie's at the sound of the siren, as she always did, and now she was with Valerie and her family plus Ben. Hank and Barbara from the diner had joined them. So first, they needed to introduce the newcomers to the travelers.

Maya looked on in astonishment at what was happening. She and Ginny had isolated themselves to be safe, and these people had gathered together to be safe. It was a completely different version of the world to her. It reminded her of Akotas' world, and she vowed that if they got through this, she would return. She belonged there, not here, and so did Ginny, even though she didn't know it yet.

How had she not understood that before, she wondered? But now she did. And whatever it took to go back with Koda, Ceya, and Pax, she would do it.

Pax nodded at her, aware that she had decided, and was grateful that part of his mission was complete. But it was a small piece. And although he still didn't understand how these people could help them, he knew they couldn't do anything until he told them the complete story.

The tornado siren eventually stopped, but the storm continued to rage around them while they all huddled in the basement, learning more about a world they had never heard of before. And at least one of them hoped he would get to visit.

Koda and Ceya filled them in on things that Pax hadn't known. And then finally Maya told them her secret. Reaching into her pocket, she took out what she had removed from the mirror in her house and held it in her hand for everyone to see.

"What is it?" Grace asked from Valerie's basement.

Ava took one look at what was in Maya's hand and turned to Evan.

"It can't be, can it?" she asked.

"It's just a stone," Lex said from Valerie's basement.

Finally, Evan asked, "What does your stone do, Maya?"

"Akotas said I could use it to return to Crann. But I don't know how to use it, so I am not sure how it helps."

Looking around the room, she saw the expression on some of their faces.

"What's happening?" Maya asked. "What's wrong?"

Ava took a deep breath before answering.

"Some of us have stones just like that, Maya, and we never really understood what they were for either. This may answer the question of why Isira sent you here."

"What do you mean some of you have stones like this?" Maya asked, closing her hand around hers.

Everyone looked to Ava to answer her question.

"It was years ago. Maybe it's just a coincidence?"

"Or it's not," Evan said. "Ava's friend Earl Wieland gave them to us before he left to go to another parallel world called Erda. We called each other the Stone Circle. But all we have ever seen them do is glow when we all got together the first time."

"What if you all have to get together again to make mine glow? Maybe that's the answer to getting back to Crann?"

"Let's hope that's not the case because two of our Stone Circle have gone to that other dimension, and two of them don't live in town anymore. Besides, how would Earl and Akotas have known each other?"

"It's possible that they did," Pax said. "I think Akotas knew how to travel between these two worlds with or without stones. He hinted at it more than once, but I didn't put it together until you said some of you have stones like Maya's."

"Still," Evan said, "We don't have all the stones."

"But I do," Grace said. "Sarah gave me hers before she left, and Eric brought back Leif's when he returned from Erda to be with me. And both Tom and Mira said the stones belonged in Doveland and gave me theirs for safekeeping."

"Well then, all we need is Ginny, and then we can test this theory," Johnny said. "Perhaps it's how we help get you all safely back to Crann."

Pax leaned back against the couch and closed his eyes. All he wanted to do was go home, and he hoped it would be that easy. But he didn't think it would be.

FORTY SEVEN

To his surprise, Fred had fallen asleep after lying awake for hours, considering his plan. He kept changing his mind.

He owned a cabin in Virginia where he had planned to take Ginny. 'Cabin' wasn't the right word because it was more like an electronic command center. Although it looked like a cabin from the outside, inside it was meticulous. Everything in the right place. Just how he liked it.

No one else had ever been inside, so nothing moved when he was away. If someone managed to break into the cabin, they wouldn't see his command center. It was underground. Upstairs it was comfortable, but not fancy, just as a cabin in the woods should look.

However, he never intended to keep someone prisoner there. It was his retreat from the world of the stupid. It was the place where he manipulated people and events behind the scenes. Doing so had made him rich.

And he would have been happy to remain behind the scenes, making things happen, trading, bargaining anonymously, but he came to hate Dradon. There was something about Dradon that made his skin crawl. It was torture sitting in the boardroom being his go-to guy. Dradon treated everyone with contempt. But he treated Fred even worse.

Everyone put up with the treatment because being part of Dradon's inner circle made them powerful and wealthy, and that's what they wanted. As Fred lay awake, he realized he wasn't any different from all of them. He wanted power and money too, and that's why he had stayed with Dradon—taking his abuse.

But something more than that must have kept him there, something he hadn't noticed. Because he didn't need to be part of their inner circle, he could have stepped away a long time ago and been wealthier and more powerful than any of them, and they would never have known.

Why didn't I do that? Fred asked himself. He had let his hatred of Dradon infect him. He had allowed himself to be Dradon's lackey, which was bad enough, but now he had betrayed him by kidnapping this woman, and Dradon would never trust him again.

If Dradon found him, he was a dead man. His entire world, the one he had built for himself, was over. Why did he fool himself into believing he could take over Dradon's empire?

Before falling asleep, that was what Fred had decided. He had been stupid. And it was time to admit it. This wasn't worth it. Perhaps it was time to take back his life.

The easiest thing to do would be to turn Ginny over to Dradon. Tell Dradon where he could find Ginny and then disappear into his own world. Dradon wouldn't find him. He could be happy.

It was the storm that woke him. The motel windows rattled, and he heard the lawn chair that had been outside their door sliding across the sidewalk.

Not a good day for traveling, he thought.

Looking across the room at Ginny, he saw she was wide awake and looking at him.

She pointed to the door with her free hand, and for a second, he wondered if she was asking him if he would let her go.

And then he heard what she must have heard. Under the screaming of the wind was a murmur of voices, and he knew what that meant.

He had made a mistake. One that he could never correct. It was too late to do anything. Dradon had found them.

· · • · ● · ● · ● · • ·

A clap of thunder covered the noise of the door breaking down, a slash of lightning highlighting a swarm of masked men in black, carrying guns in front of them as they swept into the room as if the wind sent them. Two stood by the door. Two of them grabbed Ginny, cutting the handcuffs off the bed, and dragged her out into the storm.

Fred watched her go, surprising himself with his deep desire to help her, and almost crying because he couldn't. Two other men stood over his bed, their guns pointed at him and motioned for him to get up and follow Ginny out into the storm. He slipped his shoes on and put his arms behind his back as directed.

He assumed Dradon told them not to kill him. Did that mean there was a chance to escape, or was he only alive long enough for Dradon to uncover everything he had done? He allowed himself a tiny sliver of hope, even as they pushed him out into the storm. The rain was laced with hail which hurt like small stones, except they cut too.

But he was still alive. At least for now. And he was smarter than Dradon realized he was, even though this latest plan of his was probably the worst idea he ever had. As they drove away, he saw one man close the motel door, carrying the few belongings they had left in the room, and then drive off in his car.

That was smart, Fred thought. No one would know what had happened this way.

He glimpsed Ginny's terrified face as they drove her away in another car. He was an enemy that she knew, a friend who had betrayed her. These men were something else. She had no idea what was happening to her now.

Fred couldn't let himself think about all that he had done wrong. What he had to do was plan how to get out of this. He hoped that he and Ginny were going to the same place. They probably were because Dradon would use Ginny to get him to talk. And he would. But what he would say might not be the whole truth.

As he wondered what the whole truth might be, the man in the front seat of the car turned around and stabbed him with a needle. As he felt himself slipping away, he was grateful that it was only a needle. It gave him a chance. And he was going to take it.

FORTY EIGHT

Grace decided not to go straight home after the storm. The air smelled freshly washed. The sky was a brilliant shade of blue. The entire town was awash in every shade of green imaginable. Every leaf vibrated with life. Later, the many greens would disappear, and the few dark shades of summer green would take over until fall produced a multicolored view. The beauty of it all was so breathtaking that Grace stopped walking and let it wash over her and take her away from everyday life for a moment.

It was Emily, the dance and yoga teacher, who had encouraged Grace to take up the practice of walking. Emily ran, but she told Grace that walking was just as good for her, and once she got into the habit, Grace understood it wasn't just the exercise that made walking wonderful. It was the peace it brought her.

She had heard of walking meditation and hadn't understood what it meant until she began the practice. What she discovered was that no walk was the same. Sometimes she barely dragged herself through the town. Other times she felt as if she was walking on clouds, drifting quickly from thought to thought. But always, she felt better. And that was why she decided to take a walk before going home from Valerie's. She had help now in the coffee shop, so she wasn't worried about not being there.

As she walked, Grace reflected on how much she loved the town and its people. After living a full life, she had found her permanent home. She loved that adventures came to her instead of needing to chase after them. And helping people not only made her feel more alive but also gave her a purpose. Of course, not everyone would think it was normal that they had adventures with people from other dimensions or parallel worlds the way they did, but that was the beauty of it. Even in the middle of all the dangers they often found themselves in, it still felt magical.

But then, she thought, everything around her was magical. All of nature was magical. That the world existed was magical. No one could explain all of what they saw, let alone all the things not visible to most people. There was so much more going on than the five, or maybe six, senses could see, let alone understand. Yes, life was all about magic.

The beauty of it all brought tears to her eyes as she accepted the joy of being part of this infinite life. Grace stopped to admire and breathe in the scent of her favorite lilac bush before reminding herself that she was walking, not just for pleasure, but for answers. How could they help the travelers from Crann? She was grateful that they had all eight stones, but were the stones necessary, or were they a distraction?

A second later, she felt a presence beside her, which startled her so much she stumbled. A firm hand caught her before she fell.

"I'm sorry, I didn't mean to scare you," Pax said.

"How did you do that? I didn't hear you coming,"

When Pax smiled at her, she said, "Oh, you just appeared here, didn't you?"

"I did. I'm sorry. But I wanted to speak to you before I go."

"Go? Where are you going? And why me? Will you be back?"

Pax smiled and guided Grace over to the bench used by children waiting for the school bus.

He turned to face her, holding both her hands and gazed into her deep brown eyes. It surprised Grace that his blue eyes had flecks of yellow in the iris, and wondered if everyone in Crann had eyes like that.

He looked around and then back to Grace.

"I understand why everyone loves this town. It's not as noisy as most of your world. And there are many more trees. It makes it easier to be here, but it's not my world, not my home. And I need to go home."

"Now?"

Pax looked down at their hands, then let go and swiveled on the bench to look out at the view. There was a break between the houses, and between them, he could see Emily's mountain as they called it, and before that, a large swath of forest that Ava and Evan had bought and put into trust for the town. Pax smiled at the view, thinking that if he had to stay, he could survive in Doveland, but he wouldn't be happy.

"Not now. First, I have to rescue Ginny and bring her here. I think I can do that on my own. But it would be easier if someone was with me who can do what I do. In my world, we would call you a Mother Hen. You know everyone. You see what's going on. So I came to you to make sure I was asking the right person. But even if we rescue her, Dradon will find all of you, so I need to know if you all can stop him."

Grace shivered, not from the coolness of the air, but from the memory of how many other men who acted like monsters they had dealt with in the past.

"I don't know how, but we will. We always find a way. Right now, you need to help Maya's daughter. Who did you think could help you with Ginny?"

"The one called Johnny. But I am not sure he knows what he is capable of."

"Well, if he doesn't, he will be willing to find out. And help you. It's who he is. Do you want to go ask him now?"

"No need," Pax said. "I called him."

Grace started to ask if Pax had a phone and then realized he meant he had called him a different way. A way that Johnny would hear.

Looking down the street, she saw Johnny coming towards them.

Pax stood as Johnny got nearer and waited until they were standing a few feet apart. As they stared at each other, Grace noticed how much they looked alike. Not only their looks but the way they stood. It felt as if a bubble of quiet surrounded them. They stood together as if they already knew one another. It confirmed to Grace, once again, that people meet each other who have known each other before, not only in different lifetimes but also in other worlds.

Johnny turned to Grace and helped her up from the bench.

"We'll be back. Would you let everyone know where we are going?"

"But where are you going?" Grace asked into the empty air.

For a moment, Grace let herself experience the emptiness of their going, replaced by a deep sadness she hadn't let herself feel for a long time. She missed her husband, and their going only reminded her of that longing.

Enough of that, she muttered to herself. *They are counting on me, and I won't let them down.*

Taking her phone out of her small cross-body purse, she called Valerie and then Ava. After that, she didn't know what else to do, so she started walking again, listening for answers.

FORTY NINE

Dradon stabbed at the button on his desk and yelled for his assistant. She was in his office within seconds, standing in front of his desk, eyes down, pad in hand, as he had trained her. He knew she was afraid of him. He wanted it that way, but today her fear radiated off of her in waves, and he hated her for it.

"Sir," she said, as he had taught her.

Hissing through his teeth, he told her he'd be out of the office for a few days. Cancel his meetings. As he talked, Dradon had the fleeting sensation of floating above himself, watching this mistake he was making, but he ignored it.

He knew the woman in front of him wanted to remind him that Fred was also not in the office, and there was a Board of Directors meeting that afternoon. He couldn't let her say it, couldn't let her think he wasn't in control, so he added, "Fred's with me. Cancel the board meeting. Make it two days from now."

Yes, he knew some of the board members had flown in from all over the world to be present. They were going to discuss taking over one of the largest information companies in the world. They needed his leadership to do so, his agreement, his plan. However, Dradon knew that someone else would take over if he was gone too long. He knew Fred wanted to be that person, which would never happen because he would not be gone for long. But Fred would be.

Since Fred would never be coming back, he would need another lackey to serve him. He had someone in mind—a few someones. There was always someone who believed they could take over by playing servant first. Fools, all of them. They didn't know that he was royalty in Crann, knew two worlds, not just one, and he had earned his power in this one. He had no plans to give up either his royalty or his power.

But first, he needed time to deal with Fred and to get the girl and her mother so he could travel back and forth between these two worlds. The thought of the pleasure that would bring him made his face flush, and he yelled at the girl to get out, momentarily fearful that he had shown the wrong emotion. As she backed out of the room, having practiced the ability to do so many times when Dradon wasn't there to scream at her, Dradon knew there was no need to add that if she screwed up the next few days, within the week, she and all her family would be without work, home, or money.

Dradon grabbed his suit jacket and briefcase, kicked the chair so it went spinning across the floor, and slammed the door on his way out. He wanted everyone to see his anger, to bring enough fear into their hearts that they didn't stray for a minute from the work he wanted them to do. Dradon understood it was a fine line between scaring people enough that they did what he wanted, and too much that they rebelled. He knew the line. They were frozen in fear. Just how he wanted them.

Once in his private elevator, Dradon let go of the visible anger but kept the internal one that propelled him forward into action. He had two people to attend to; one to win over, one to destroy.

It was going to be a good day.

• • • • ● • ● • ● • • •

Neither Fred nor Ginny shared Dradon's point of view. So far, it had been the worst day of both their lives, but both of them, for different reasons, were grateful that they were at least in the same room and could talk to each other.

Fred, knowing why they were there, also understood why they were alone together. Dradon wanted him to tell Ginny what was going on. It would save him the trouble of convincing Ginny to side with Dradon to save her mother.

So, even though Fred recognized it would serve Dradon, Fred also realized he needed to tell her what was happening. He could not leave her defenseless.

The room was dark, but the light from a window high on one wall provided him with enough light to see Ginny. They were strapped into chairs, facing each other.

He had woken to Ginny staring at him, and as he opened his eyes, she asked him if he was alright and then waited.

What kind of person did that? Fred asked himself. He had lied to her, kidnapped her, and gotten her into this situation, and the first thing she asks is if he is alright.

He waited a long beat before deciding how to answer.

"I'm sorry."

Ginny cocked her head, staring at him, registering the truth of what he said, and then dropped her head back and looked at the ceiling, trying to compose herself. She blinked back her tears. She reminded herself that she had no time to be sorry for herself. She had to get out of this situation and find her mother.

Taking a deep breath, she said, "Tell me what's going on. You owe me that at least."

As Fred explained what he knew about Dradon and what Dradon had asked him to do and why, Ginny let herself cry. First silent tears, and then racking sobs, crying so hard she couldn't breathe. Fred wanted to comfort her, but there were no words that would make it better. Finally, she took a ragged breath and asked, "Why didn't my mother tell me?"

"She was afraid and was trying to protect you."

"What's going to happen now?"

"I'm sure Dradon is on the way. He'll take you and get rid of me. I don't know why he wants you so much. I only know that he will use you and your mother to get what he wants."

Fred saw Ginny's face flush, her eyes red from crying, tears still dripping from her chin as she composed herself before speaking.

"Then, I'm sorry, too. Why didn't you simply ask for my help? Why not tell me this instead of lying to me and putting us both in this position. I would have listened. I would have helped."

Fred looked at Ginny and realized she was telling the truth. He had been wrong. Utterly wrong about everything. The only thing he had done right was have the intention of taking over Dradon's company. But for all the wrong reasons.

Both of them fell silent, waiting for what would happen next. Nothing left to say.

Ginny realized she would do what Dradon asked of her to save her mother. Perhaps she could bargain for Fred's life in the process. Fred was thinking the same thing. Did he have anything he could use to negotiate with Dradon to save Ginny and her mother?

In that silence, two men appeared in the room. Fred and Ginny were too shocked to do anything but stare.

"Sh..." one of them said, as they each worked on the straps that held them to their chairs.

One man wrapped his arms around Fred and the other around Ginny. Ginny had only a moment to notice that he had blue eyes with yellow flecks before the room fell away.

FIFTY

D radon arrived moments later. The guards unlocked the door, and Dradon stepped inside the room, expecting to see Fred and Ginny. The men who came in with him stood stunned and then froze in fear as Dradon roared his anger, turned to both of them, grabbed them, and threw them against the wall. They barely had time to register that the stories they'd heard about Dradon's freaky strength were true before he kicked them both in the head, rendering them incapable of any further thoughts in this lifetime.

Even as he unleashed his fury upon them, Dradon recognized it wasn't their fault. They couldn't have known about people who could appear and disappear in a room without opening doors. But it didn't matter. They had failed him.

Not for the first time, Dradon wished he, too, could transport himself where he wanted to go on a whim. Instead, he needed to use the transportation that the peons of this world used to get to the town he'd ignored because he didn't consider it worth bothering with.

But it had to be the people of that town who'd saved Ginny and Fred. And the only reason they would have known to do so was that someone from Crann was in this world. He had been right.

But who was it? And now that they were here, perhaps he could force them to take him to Crann.

Maybe I don't need Maya and Ginny anymore, Dradon thought. But only for a moment. He knew he had to get rid of the two of them anyway. Otherwise, the people in Crann would choose them over him.

Staring at the lifeless forms of the two guards, Dradon made a decision.

He would go to the town with the stupid name. Perhaps he would reason with them, explain his plan, offer them riches and power beyond their wildest dreams. And if that didn't work, destroy them. How powerful could they be? They were mere mortals.

Dradon spit on the ground, thinking about how he knew about Doveland. His father and Akotas. If Akotas were still alive, he would pay for this. If not, his family would. That was almost as good.

Sliding into the back seat of the car, Dradon yelled directions at the driver as he slammed the door. Just thinking about his father made him furious. The promises he hadn't kept. At least not to him.

Their father had traveled between worlds in the same way that other people took trips to other countries. He promised to teach his children how to travel too, but first, they needed to earn the right to do so. It was not something to be taken lightly. There were rules to follow, so every world remained safe. Not surprisingly, their father decided Dradon had not earned that right. But he had taught Akotas and Isira long before they all fell off the cliff together.

Isira wasn't interested in visiting other parallel worlds, but Akotas was curious and visited this one more than once. When he came home, he would share his adventures with Isira but never with him.

It didn't matter. Dradon always found ways to hear about what Akotas found. Dradon knew that during one of his trips, Akotas met a man named Earl. Earl and his wife, Ariel, were also from another parallel world. Akotas and Earl became friends and Earl told Akotas about the people that they were gathering who possessed unique gifts and about the town those people would move to after he and his wife returned to their dimension. It was a sister village to their village in Crann and they could always go there to get help if they needed it.

And that's how Dradon learned about Doveland. And that, Dradon knew, had to be where Fred and Ginny were now.

As Dradon's anger cooled, he realized that perhaps this would work out in his favor after all. Now everyone would be together in one place, and he could use them to get what he wanted.

"Drive faster," Dradon shouted. One of the men in the front seat put the blue flashing light on the roof, and the other switched on the siren.

Not for the first time, Dradon wished he'd inherited his brother and sister's powers. But he hadn't. However, he had an ability that no one knew about--including them--and that was the one he'd unleash this time, in full view of everyone. It would scare them into inaction, or he'd use it to stop them forever. Either way was okay with him.

Soon he'd be back in Crann. He couldn't wait.

"Faster," he screamed.

The men in the front seat grimaced. They were going as fast as they could. They hoped it was fast enough for the crazy man in the back seat, because otherwise, they were dead men when it was over. There was no point in trying to stop him. Dradon made it clear to everyone that worked for him that he had people who would carry out orders to eliminate anyone's family if they disobeyed him or if something happened to him.

No one knew whether or not he could, but then, no one wanted to take that chance.

• • • ● ● • ● • • •

After the storm, Isira had walked back to the cliff, not aware of anything other than that Pax hadn't returned. Perhaps it was time to accept that he had failed. Which meant she would need to find Ginny and Maya herself. But if she died too, what would happen to their world? Would Dradon make his way back? If he did, he would destroy everything.

Isira moved to the extreme edge of the cliff and sat down, feeling the sharp stones dig into her thighs, her feet hanging over the void. She knew it was a dangerous thing to do. A strong wind could knock her over the edge. But maybe that was what she was waiting for. Fate to step in and decide for her.

As she lifted her tear-streaked face to the brilliant blue sky to say goodbye in case she never came back, she felt a hand on her shoulder, and then someone lifted her up and away from the cliff.

"You don't need to go, Isira," she heard in a familiar voice.

Turning, she flung herself in the man's arms and sobbed.

"Akotas, I thought you had gone forever."

"I'm sorry," he said, leaning over so his forehead rested on his sister's head.

"I'm sorry," he said again as he stepped back and held onto his sister's shoulders, looking into her eyes. "I should have told you."

"Why didn't you?" Isira asked as they walked away from the cliff and sat down together on the log they used as a bench.

"It was for Pax and the future of our people," Akotas said, holding her hand.

"Tell me," Isira said.

FIFTY ONE

I should be used to this, Ava said to herself, as she held on to the nearest chair so she wouldn't fall over from the shock of seeing four people materialize in her living room.

"Help," Pax said.

Recovering, Ava rushed to get the woman who was slumped in Pax's arms. Pax moved to Johnny to help with the man he was keeping from collapsing to the ground.

As Ava assisted the woman to the sofa, Maya ran into the living room with Koda and Ceya behind her, screaming, "Ginny!"

"Mom," Ginny sobbed as the two women clutched each other, rocking back and forth on the couch.

Ava gestured with her head, and Johnny and Pax pulled Fred out to the patio and sat him in one of the chairs.

Too shocked to struggle against what was happening, Fred finally managed to ask, "Where am I? How did I get here?"

Koda pulled a chair closer to Fred, knees touching, and stared. What he saw wasn't impressive—a small, balding, middle-aged man, glasses that hid his pale blue eyes—and wondered how this man had enticed Akotas' daughter to follow him.

"It's because she doesn't know who she is," Ceya said, knowing what Koda was thinking.

"Well, it's time we told her," Koda responded.

"I agree," Maya said from the doorway, her arm around her daughter.

"What do we do with him?" Koda asked, gesturing to Fred.

Fred trembled. He had thought he was frightened before, but the fear he felt now was so intense he couldn't breathe.

It surprised him when he felt Ginny's hand on his back as she pushed his head forward between his knees, whispering, "It's okay."

Shaking his head, hanging below his knees, Fred answered, "It's not okay. It will never be okay."

Then, to his shock and embarrassment, Fred did something he had never done before. He started weeping. Ginny pulled a chair up beside him and, her hand circling his back, whispered again, "It's okay."

As she put aside all the fear and anger she had felt towards him, Ginny realized Fred wasn't any different from some of the children in her classroom. He was hurt, and he had lashed out. The only difference was he was an adult and should have known better. But then, what if no one had ever said to him, "It's okay," and given him a moment of safety?

Pax stood apart from everyone, letting his strength return. He glanced at Johnny, and the two of them smiled at each other, knowing what the other was going through. Then Johnny did the strangest thing. He winked at him, and then looked at Ginny comforting Fred.

Puzzled at the wink, Pax wondered what it meant. Birds had winked at him before, but never a person. He understood it was a message. But what did it mean?

While Ginny comforted Fred and everyone else stood observing, Ava and Evan returned to the kitchen to make coffee. As the coffee dripped into the pot and Evan warmed up muffins in the microwave, Ava observed each person on the patio. Pax and Johnny leaning against the supports of the overhanging roof. Ginny leaning over Fred. Maya standing over the two of them. Koda and Ceya pressed together, fingers touching, eyes glinting with occasional flashes of red, giving the impression of choosing whether to pounce or to fly.

Hank stood outside the group, also watching. But Ava knew he was scanning for danger and she was watching for understanding. Hank looked up and smiled at her. The two of them were there because they had been given second chances. Did this Fred person deserve one, and if he did, what would that look like?

• • • ● • ● • • •

"Tell me what?" Ginny asked.

Even though over an hour had gone by since Ceya had spoken, everyone knew what she meant.

Everyone except Fred was in the living room. Grace, Valerie, and Craig had arrived, leaving Lex to watch Ben at their house. Bryan and Rachel sat together on the couch, Rachel's hand on Bryan's bouncing knee.

Hank had put Fred in another room, handcuffed to the bed, and Fred almost laughed at the irony of it. Now he was the one handcuffed to a bed. What was intriguing to him was how peaceful he felt about it. After being magically transported somewhere, weeping in front of strangers, being treated with compassion by Ginny and at least tolerated by everyone else, something inside of him had twisted around.

What had happened was not at all how the world was supposed to look. Fred lay back on the bed, staring at the ceiling. The door to the room was closed, and what looked like a baby monitor was in the room with him. He assumed the other end was in with the others. He couldn't hear them, but they would hear him if he tried to escape.

They didn't need to worry. Fred had no desire to escape. A breeze blew through the open window, sending the sheer white curtains billowing out into the room. The bed was comfortable, and for the moment, he was safe. There was nothing he could do about anything. The relief was so enormous, Fred sighed with the pleasure of it and let himself drift away into sleep.

Out in the living room, Ginny waited for the answer to her question. Maya cleared her throat, looked to Pax for support, and began the story of how she had met a man who had fallen out of nowhere and had fallen in love with him the moment she saw him.

Pax watched Ginny as her mother explained her heritage. He saw her eyes widen, her face flush, her glances at Koda and Ceya as she learned who they were. And finally, she looked at him.

At that moment, Pax understood two things. Why it needed to be him that came to this world, and what the wink meant.

FIFTY TWO

As the car sped towards Doveland, Dradon forced himself to become calm and detached. He understood his rage would not provide him with answers. And he needed answers. Where were Maya and Ginny? Yes, he knew they must be in Doveland, but where exactly? How would he get them away from their rescuers? Who were these rescuers, anyway? Who was it who had come from Crann? How many of them?

The less critical questions like what to do with Fred, Dradon would leave till later. He'd have the two men driving the car keep Fred imprisoned until he could decide what to do about him.

By the time one man said, "Thirty minutes, sir," Dradon was ready. He had a plan, and he was sure it would work because no one but his brother knew about the one power he had, and Dradon was positive that Akotas was not the one who came to rescue Ginny and Maya.

Akotas was too much of a coward. Too busy taking care of their clan to worry about his wife and child. Dradon had proof. Akotas had left Maya and Ginny to fend for themselves in this world when Akotas knew perfectly well that Dradon would come after them, eventually.

The time was now. And he had the element of surprise. Whoever they were, they would know he was coming, but they wouldn't know what he could do.

Only Akotas would.

Once again, Dradon assured himself that Akotas was not in Doveland because he would have felt his presence if he were. Besides, he's probably dead, Dradon told himself.

He leaned back into the car seat built explicitly for his comfort, closed his eyes, and moved his thoughts out, searching for the people from Crann. As the miles passed, the signal became clearer. Four people from Crann. Dradon reasoned that Ginny was one of them since she had been born on Crann. And, of course, Maya would be with her, but Maya was no match for him. That meant there were only three travelers from Crann he needed to deal with. Easy.

"Where to?" the driver asked.

Dradon gave him directions and then smiled to himself. They would see him coming, of course, but that didn't provide them with the advantage. The advantage belonged to him. He was unique. He was better than they were. He had always known this truth about himself. And soon the people in Doveland, and the ones from Crann, would learn the truth too.

Dradon closed his eyes, dreaming of Crann and returning there as the powerful leader and ruler, which was his birthright. With all the people from Crann under his control, returning would be easy. He wouldn't need Maya and Ginny anymore. The other three must know the secret to traveling between worlds, otherwise they wouldn't have come.

Soon he would have the secret too, and everything he ever wanted would be his. It was only a matter of time.

· • ● · ● · ● · • ·

"Did you bring the stones?" Evan asked.

Grace reached into her purse and pulled out a small box that she had brought with her when she moved to Doveland. It used to hold jewelry. Now the box held the stones that Sarah, Leif, Tom, and Mira left in her safekeeping. She took them out one by one and laid them on the coffee table by the couch, where they looked like four ordinary rocks smoothed out by a stream. There were no markings on them that told anyone to whom they belonged or why they were unique.

Johnny laid his stone on the table, as did Ava, Evan, and Craig. Maya reached into her pocket and took out hers. She reluctantly placed her stone on the table, being careful to keep it slightly separate in case it had nothing to do with the rest of them. This stone had been in her keeping all these years, and she had never looked at it after Akotas put it into the mirror frame. Now she realized it looked like any ordinary rock. Maybe it meant nothing at all.

All nine stones sat on the table. Nothing happened.

"Now what?" Ginny asked.

"Now we wait," Koda answered.

A long pause settled over the room.

It was Ginny who broke the silence by asking, "Where's Pax?"

FIFTY THREE

Pax knew what he was about to do was crazy. But the minute he really looked at Ginny, he understood what he needed to do. Akotas and Isira had sent him to this world for a purpose. No, he didn't fit here, but then he barely fit into Crann. Learning he was a descendant of William Sky and that was the reason he looked and acted differently only softened the hurt of being different, and in some ways, it made it worse.

William Sky was a hero. He was only a boy, maybe a man now, who loved to live at the top of the Tree Of Life by himself and with the owl who hooted at him each morning. When Akotas left, he missed him as if someone had removed an arm from his body. But he had adjusted and been at peace with his life.

But Akotas' memory would never let him alone. He could hear Akotas saying, "You have a purpose, Pax. Everyone has a purpose in this world. No one is the same as anyone else. That's how it's supposed to be. Each of us fits into the tapestry of life and makes it whole."

"Not me," Pax would say, until he learned it was better to keep that thought to himself because it would upset Akotas. Sometimes it made Akotas angry. But what was much worse was when Pax could see that somehow saying that wounded Akotas, and he would become sad and withdrawn.

Despite Pax's stubbornness, Akotas always came back and fulfilled his role as Pax's teacher. It was the coming back that taught Pax the most important lesson. He could fail, be hurt, and afraid, and still return to do what he needed to do.

When he saw all nine stones lying on the table, doing nothing, he understood. He didn't add the stone Akotas gave him to the table because he realized the stones would not stop Dradon. He had to do it. His survival wasn't important. What was important was that peace remained in Crann and that Ginny and her mother could return with Koda and Ceya and be safe in the place he loved.

Before leaving, he stole one last glance at Ginny sitting on the couch with Maya, already looking like the High Priestess she would be. Kind, gentle, and brave, Ginny would bring even deeper peace to his people, and Isira would be free to move on. Perhaps Akotas had waited for her, and they would rule another world in another lifetime together.

With that thought, Pax left to find Dradon, praying he would be strong enough to stop him, determined he would no matter the cost. Akotas had taught him to be a warrior. But not with weapons made of steel or bone. He would use the weapon of truth told and defended.

• • • • ● • ● • ● • • •

Outside of Doveland, a field of wildflowers bloomed. It had once been the farm that belonged to a man named Jay Kalen. His wife and daughter had died in a fire, and he had died not long after having drunk himself to death in his grief.

Thirty years later, Jay had returned, a new man, born again into another body but with all the memories of the man he had been before.

It was in that field that Jay had died again, and in the process, saved the town of Doveland from the man who had killed so many in the name of power.

Pax had heard the field calling him while sitting in the woods outside Ava's house that morning. It told him it was a good place to die, and Pax had agreed.

So it was near that field when Pax revealed himself to Dradon in the back seat of his car. To Dradon's credit, he did not flinch or yell but breathed in and out slowly and then smiled.

"So you are the one," Dradon said.

In the front seat, the passenger turned around and said, "Sir?"

Dradon glared at him. Turning back around, the driver looked at the passenger and rolled his eyes. The passenger shrugged. There was a slight chance the man in the back seat was going crazy, and they would be rid of him forever. Perhaps he was crazy. But crazy didn't save them.

"Don't talk out loud," Pax mind-spoke to Dradon.

Dradon nodded. He'd never done it before, but perhaps it would work, so he thought the question.

"You are the one, aren't you?"

"The one what?"

"The one Akotas sent to stop me. And if you are, how do you plan to do it?"

"Let's talk about it," Pax said. "Ask the driver to pull over."

"Here? It's a field!"

"Tell them you need a moment to yourself to think something over."

Dradon shrugged. This person was someone he would have to get rid of, anyway. He might as well do it before they got to Doveland. Besides, he was curious. The best thing that could happen is this boy-man could show him how to get to Crann and back, and that would solve all his problems. The worse, he'd have to spend a little energy to get rid of him.

"Pull over."

"Sir?"

"Pull over," he shouted to the driver. "I need a moment to think by myself."

Pax had seen a bench at the side of the meadow, dedicated to the man Jay Kalen, so that's where he walked to with Dradon. At the top of a small rise, it couldn't be seen from the car and the men waiting for Dradon. Sheltered under a tree and looking out over the waving fields, it was a peaceful place. Looking up, Pax could see the metal silver bird called an airplane, and he knew he would never ride in one.

Dradon sat and waited.

"You seem to be a brave young man."

"Perhaps," Pax said. "Maybe even foolish, but I can't let you go on into Doveland."

Dradon threw his head back and laughed.

"How do you plan to stop me?"

"I'll make you a deal," Pax replied. "You want the secret of traveling between worlds, and I know it. But you will have to fight me to get it."

Dradon laughed again and turned to look at the man on the bench beside him. A tiny voice spoke to him to be cautious, but he ignored it. How could this person fight him?

"It's a deal. I win, you tell me. You win, what happens?"

"You stop," Pax said.

Dradon stood. Pax remained seated.

Dradon smiled, turned on his secret power. The power that had brought him wealth beyond measure, that had moved peaceful men into men of war, and destroyed those that opposed him and waited.

The man on the bench lifted his blue eyes to Dradon, smiled, and said, "That's it?"

It took every ounce of Pax's strength not to reveal that he could feel his insides melting. That his head felt as if it would explode. That within moments, the person known as Pax would be nothing other than an empty shell, and Ginny, her mother, and all of Crann would fall to this man.

Pax called to the trees, the meadow, to every creature of nature, and asked for help. He opened his heart to the wind, the sun, and the clouds floating above him and became one with them.

Blades of grass tipped towards him. The yellow of the last daffodils flashed in and out as they moved with the wind. He felt the seat beneath him move in waves, no longer solid.

His feet on the earth expanded, filling out through the meadow, sending shoots down, down, down into the earth, as the top of his head opened up, and a cloud filled the space where he used to be.

With a whisper of his last breath, Pax smiled at Dradon and said, "You lose."

FIFTY FOUR

Pax's disappearance from Ava's living room was not a surprise to Koda and Ceya. He had gone to do what he needed to do. It would have been better if he had asked them to come with him, but that he went alone didn't surprise them.

But for everyone else, it was a moment of terror. Then the ground shook. And stopped. Everyone stood expecting there to be more, but there wasn't. Looking around the living room, they noticed nothing had moved or fallen. Even the stones had not moved on the table.

"What was that?" Hank demanded, not really expecting an answer but feeling as if he had to do something.

Koda and Ceya looked at each other. Was that something Pax did?

"We don't know," they answered together.

Evan walked outside to see if there was any damage and the group followed, milling around, looking for answers. And Pax.

· · · • · • · • · ·

Moments before the ground shook, Bryan had reached for Rachel's hand and whispered, "We need to go." He motioned to Johnny to come with them, and they were standing by the car when it happened.

Bryan turned to Johnny and asked, "Can you take us somewhere?"

Johnny nodded.

Turning to Rachel, Bryan said, "Johnny and I need to leave now. Meet us at the meadow near Jay's bench."

"You want me to take you there now?" Johnny asked.

Bryan nodded. Johnny touched Bryan's shoulder, and they both vanished, leaving Rachel standing by the car by herself.

Rachel's breath hitched as they disappeared, and she muttered to herself, "That's okay, Rach. People come and go in thin air all the time."

· · · ● · ● · ● · · ·

Johnny brought them both to Jay's bench, his hand still on Bryan's shoulder. They sat, grateful that it was there.

"Thanks," Bryan said, waiting for his head to stop spinning. "This couldn't wait."

Johnny blinked, afraid to nod in case it made his head fall off. It was a strange feeling, but he knew it would pass. Learning that he could bring someone with him as he transported himself didn't actually please him. Doing it at all wasn't as wonderful as people who hadn't done it thought it would be.

There were moments of being nowhere and hoping he'd end up where he meant to go. But what if he didn't? What if he got lost?

That was something he tried not to think about, and now that they were where Bryan wanted to go, he could let the fear go for the moment. But he knew he would revisit the whole transport-into-nothingness-and-back-again once this adventure was over.

He was happy that Rachel was on her way so that they could get back to the house in a more conventional and definitely less terrifying way.

Looking around, he saw nothing but the meadow, and he didn't understand why they were there when Bryan grabbed his arm and pulled him up.

"I need you to see this too," Bryan said.

Johnny knew that meant he had to keep touching Bryan to see why they there were there, so he put his hand on his arm and waited.

Seconds later, he flinched and moved back. Bryan put his hand on Johnny's, keeping them connected, and stepped forward.

Johnny took a deep breath and looked at the man staring at them with hatred in his eyes and a rage so fierce it radiated off of him in waves. Part of him felt like hating him, and the other part was willing to do whatever this man would ask of him. It was a terrifying feeling. Only the awareness that the man was in the in-between kept him from bowing down in fear.

"I'm not going," Dradon yelled, stepping closer to the two of them. Johnny could feel Bryan shaking, even though he stood his ground.

"You are already gone," Bryan responded. "Now you have a choice."

Dradon stomped, raised his fists, and moved even closer.

Johnny did his best not to flinch.

"Fix this, or I'll haunt you forever. You, your family, your friends."

Bryan smiled, and although he looked calm, Johnny could feel Bryan's hand tremble, and he understood why Bryan needed him there.

"That is an empty threat, Dradon. You have no power in this place."

Johnny wondered if that was true, but he kept his eyes on the man, doing his best not to let his fear show.

"Let me show you where you are now," Bryan said, walking forward into the meadow, Johnny holding onto his arm, trying not to stumble.

Reluctantly, Dradon followed.

"Look down there," Bryan said, leaning forward slightly so that Johnny could see, too.

A crack ran through the meadow. One he had never seen before. Just wide enough to slip through. At the bottom, he glimpsed the man who stood before them. Still. Unmoving. Dead.

"No!" Dradon shouted. "I'm not going!"

Bryan repeated once again, "You are already gone."

As they watched, the ground trembled, and the crack in the meadow closed, sealing in the man at the bottom.

"No!" Dradon wailed. "Bring me back!"

Bryan waited until Dradon turned to face him.

"You know no one can bring you back. Here are your choices. Stay in this in-between, powerless, or move on. I'm here to help you move on. But if you don't do it now, I won't help, and you will be stuck like this forever or end up where you don't want to go."

Turning his back on Dradon, Bryan walked back to Jay's bench and sat down, with Johnny by his side.

"Now what?" Johnny whispered.

"We wait," Bryan said. "This should be interesting."

A few moments later, Johnny saw what Bryan meant.

Dradon, standing alone in the field, raised his fists and swore at the sky. Moments later, a black cloud emerged from the cloudless sky. It settled above Dradon, blocking the sun. A dark whirl of wind filled with sticks and leaves rose from the ground surrounding Dradon, expanding until it reached the cloud. It was over in seconds. The cloud disappeared, the leaves and sticks dropped to the ground, and Dradon had vanished.

"What happened?" Johnny whispered.

"He chose," Bryan said.

FIFTY FIVE

Rachel saw the two men on the bench, and her breath caught in her throat. They were so still. Were they okay? Then Bryan turned and smiled at her, and her heart soared as it did every time he looked at her.

Reaching the bench, she sat down beside Bryan and held his hand. The meadow was glowing. Wildflowers and grasses moving with the wind, reflecting the sun back to itself.

The three of them sat for a long minute together, listening to the bird songs.

"He's gone," Bryan said.

"Who?" Rachel asked.

"Pax. He's gone."

"I'm sorry," Rachel said. "I know you wanted to get to know him better."

Bryan nodded, trying to hold back tears.

"But so is that man, and that had to be what Pax came to do," Johnny added, marveling at the sacrifice Pax had made. Would Ginny understand all the reasons he did it?

Rachel put her arm around Bryan, not knowing what to say to make it better. She knew he had hoped to spend more time in the woods with Pax. Rachel also suspected that Bryan had also hoped to visit Pax's world somehow.

The sun beat down on her head, making her lightheaded. She wondered why there weren't any clouds over the meadow, although she could see them further out. Another mystery she couldn't solve at that moment.

"Can we go now?" she asked. "People back at the house will be worried. And there are two men sitting in the car at the bottom of the rise, waiting for someone named Dradon. Is that who you mean by 'that man?'"

Bryan and Johnny looked at each other. "What do we tell them?"

"We don't tell them anything. We bring them someone else," Johnny answered.

· · · ● · ● · ● · · ·

"Will this work?" Grace asked. "Why should we let Fred go? How do we know he won't be as bad as that man, Dradon?"

Rachel, Bryan, and Johnny had returned to the house and explained the situation and the plan.

Before leaving the meadow, they told the two men in the car that there was no one in the meadow. Perhaps the man they were waiting for had left?

"How?" The driver had sneered at her. "We've been here the entire time. No one but you came through here." Looking at Bryan and Johnny, he added, "He must have met you two since you must have been here before us. You better explain yourself. Where is he?"

Rachel tipped her head and smiled up at him as if this were an ordinary conversation with one of her clients. She gestured at Bryan and Johnny and said, "My friends went on a hike. Then these lazy butts didn't feel like walking back to town, so they called me to pick them up. But that's it. I know they didn't see anyone once they got here. I heard a helicopter as I was driving here. Perhaps your friend left that way?"

Rachel smiled again at the two men in the car. She had taken off her sunglasses so she could look directly at them, and she hoped the terror that extended from the bottom of her feet to the top of her head was not showing in her eyes.

"Sorry about that. I wish we could be of more help. Perhaps your friend expected you to know he was leaving that way."

"He told us to wait. We'll wait."

"Well, if you are hungry or thirsty while you wait, there is a lovely diner and coffee shop in town."

The driver squinted his eyes, looked at the other man, and then said again, "We'll wait here."

"Suit yourself," Rachel said, trying not to give away the lie.

Back at the house, Johnny explained the plan to the group. He would take Fred to the meadow. Fred would weave a story that would explain the situation to the men in the car and later to the world. What Fred came up with wasn't their business. It was Fred's problem.

The question Grace was asking was not only would it work, but was it the right thing to do?

"Yes, how do we know Fred will do the right thing?" Hank asked.

Hank had brought Fred out of the bedroom and sat beside him at the table, watching him like a hawk. Although Hank believed Fred was too smart to run, there was always the chance he thought he could get away with it.

As Hank asked his question, he stared at the man beside him, wishing he could see into him and figure out what he would do.

"Second chances," Ava replied.

"I agree," Ginny said. "Perhaps some good will come out of this. It will take someone as conniving and clever as Fred to explain away Dradon's absence and handle the people who followed him.

Besides, I don't want to be in the punishment business. Technically, all he did was kidnap me. And it wasn't that big a deal, anyway. He thought he was doing the right thing. I think he can do the right thing now."

Fred observed the discussion as if he was another person. He only understood a little of what was going on. Enough to realize that somehow Dradon was gone forever, and they were giving him a chance to fix the mess Dradon had made.

He would have his dream come true. He would run Dradon's company and perhaps make it into one that didn't take advantage of everyone. It would take a while to turn it around, but he figured he could do it.

Taking advantage of the silence that followed Grace's question, Fred asked what happened to Dradon.

"He took the wrong path," Johnny said.

"Will he return?"

"No."

"Are you sure?"

"Positive," Bryan sighed. He was happy no one asked in front of Fred where Pax had gone. Even Koda and Ceya had remained silent. But seeing their faces, Bryan had a feeling that they knew. Perhaps they would tell him. All he knew for sure is that it was because of Pax that Dradon would never return, which set Ginny and Maya free. Finding out what that meant would have to wait until they took care of this problem.

Hank turned to Fred and said, "Make up the story you want to tell. Make it stick. But remember, we will be watching you."

Hank was not quite ready to believe that this would work. But like everyone else, he wanted it to.

"It's agreed then," Ava asked.

"Yes," each member of the Doveland Karass said one by one, some with more confidence than others.

Koda, Ceya, Maya, and Ginny stood to the side, waiting, knowing that this part of the problem was not something they could solve.

Maya squeezed Ginny's hand. She didn't know where Pax had gone, but Maya recognized that her daughter missed him already.

Johnny reached over to Fred, touched him on the shoulder, and they both vanished.

Valerie sighed. She understood what these trips were costing Johnny. But she also knew her son's heart. It was something he had to do.

FIFTY SIX

Johnny returned moments later, looking even more drained than Valerie worried he would be. She rushed to his side and held him close until he could speak.

"It's done. I left Fred in the meadow to figure out what he would say. What happens next is in his hands. Even if he tries to tell the story of what he has heard and seen, who will believe him? To save his own life, he will need to tell a story people will accept."

"But will he be another Dradon?" Hank asked. Yes, Hank believed in second chances, but he didn't know the man.

"No," Ginny said. "There is a good heart in there somewhere. Besides, he wants to make things better. It might not be our way, but it will be better than it was."

A long silence filled the room.

It was Koda who broke it.

"And there was no sign of Pax?"

Johnny shook his head.

Rachel thought about missing clouds over the meadow and wondered if they were part of the story of Pax's disappearance.

"Maybe he went back to Crann?" she asked.

"He wouldn't have left without Ginny and Maya unless he didn't have a choice," Koda said. "He gave himself up to save all of us from Dradon."

Ginny stood beside her mother, not caring that everyone saw the tears streaming down her face. She had hoped to get to know him, and now she would never have the chance.

"Pax also came here to take the two of you back to Crann. He would want us to do that. Are you willing to go?"

"But, do you know how?" Maya asked.

Before Koda could answer her there was a flash of light at the edge of the forest, and Ginny, who had been looking in that direction, screamed, "Mom!"

Maya didn't answer. Instead, she ran straight towards the light. She'd seen it before. She knew what it meant.

FIFTY SEVEN

I t was still dark when Grace stepped outside for her walk. While lying in her bed, she had heard the call of the cardinal through her open window. She knew he was waking the bird community, but it worked for her too. She needed to walk. And think. And fully embrace what had happened after Akotas arrived the day before.

Maya had run towards the flash of light, Ginny had run after her mother, and Koda and Ceya had followed. Everyone else moved outside to observe what was happening, but not to interfere. Even now, Grace couldn't really comprehend what they experienced. Two worlds came together for a moment in time. The entire adventure was over within a few days.

But Grace wanted more. Grace realized she wasn't the only one that mourned that it was over. Bryan and Johnny almost wept as they watched the travelers leave. Akotas put his arms around Maya and Ginny, reached out to Koda and Ceya, and they all disappeared together, leaving a void in the hearts of everyone else.

As Grace walked, the sky lightened, and birds sang as the sun peeped over the horizon, the robins filling the morning with their constant song.

It will be a beautiful day for our Mother's Day gathering, Grace thought.

Looking up at the trees, the morning light filtering through the leaves, Grace marveled at the beauty of the world around her, and like Bryan, she wished she could see the other world that treasured that beauty more than this world did.

Her phone beeped, and she saw a message from Ava to everyone. "Let's meet at the meadow instead of our house."

Within a few minutes, everyone had responded they would be there. No one was sleeping in this morning, Grace realized. After the adventure of the last few days, probably everyone was having the same trouble sleeping that she was.

She texted back that she would be there too and turned back towards her home. She had scones to make. Maybe baking would take away some of her sadness. Because that's what she realized she felt. She felt bereft. People she had wanted to know better had left, leaving behind more questions than answers.

· · · ● · ● · ● · ● ·

Bryan was walking, too, not being able to sleep. He walked, hardly paying attention to anything around him. The rabbit kept stopping and looking back at him, making sure he was still coming.

Oh, yea, Bryan said to himself. *I'm still coming. What other choice do I have?*

He knew that the way he was walking through the woods bothered the rabbit. But today, the woods meant nothing to him. Instead of it filling him with joy, he felt like a wooden soldier doing his duty. But that's what he did, his duty. So what?

So Bryan let the rabbit pull him forward, the bird songs sounding louder than usual as if they were trying to break through the wall he had built around himself the moment he realized Pax was no longer in this world. He didn't want to feel the wave of sadness that had engulfed him. Pax had been someone who understood the woods better than he did, and he had only known him for a moment. He needed more time.

Then all the visitors were gone. And the stones that were supposed to be the answer remained still and silent on the coffee table.

They had all stared at them for a moment, and then Johnny said, "So these stones mean nothing?"

Bryan had turned and walked out of the house. Somehow Rachel got him to the car and had driven them home. He was barely functioning. It felt as if something had sucked away the magic they experienced the last few days.

Not thinking, just moving his feet, Bryan followed the rabbit to the clearing where he and Pax had talked. Plopping himself down, Bryan leaned against a tree and closed his eyes. Openly weeping now. Shocking himself. Thinking that perhaps he was making up for all the times he held it together.

He felt, rather than heard, the question, "Why the sadness, my friend."

Bryan stood, looked. There was nothing. And then a slight pulse, the barest whisper of movement, and a figure so transparent he could see the trees behind him.

"Pax?" Bryan whispered.

A few hours later, Pax said, "You'll explain to them?"

Bryan nodded, not trusting himself to speak, and then tried to smile as the pulse, the whisper in the wind, faded away, and he was left with a stone clutched in his hand.

FIFTY EIGHT

"He explained the stones?" Johnny asked.

All the adults sat together on blankets near Jay's bench. Almost where the crack in the ground had been just a day before. Close to the place where they were having another picnic the day Jay Kalen saved Hank's life. Hank's heart always felt both lighter and heavier when they came to this meadow.

Looking at Jay's bench, he realized they would need to add another one for Pax. One man from another lifetime, and the other from another world. Hank realized he did not see symbols as easily as others did, but this one was hard to miss.

And he was grateful that it was in this meadow where they were celebrating Mother's Day. Because the celebration reminded him they weren't just celebrating human mother and child, but the children of animals, flowers, grasses. The whole of the planet called Gaia was a mother. Perhaps all the universes were the same.

"More likely than not," Johnny whispered to Hank. "Sorry, I couldn't help but hear your thoughts about this place. It seems to have that effect."

Hank patted Johnny on the back. He was so proud of him. Johnny was the son he never had. In fact, all the people surrounding him became his family after he and Ava found each other. His nephew Ben raced through the meadow, Lex laughing as he followed him, making sure he remained safe. Everyone watched out for each other in this family, this Karass.

Grace sat beside Rachel on a blanket and felt as if she were floating on air. She had told no one, but she too had a visit from Pax that morning. At the end of her walk, she stopped in the park, sat on the bench that faced the Diner and her shop, and wondered what was the point of it all. She'd been through these feelings before. Sometimes they lasted longer than others. She hoped the feeling would fade quickly this time.

Suddenly she had felt the pulse that Bryan had described, and then a slight whiff of wind and a presence she couldn't see but only sensed sat on the bench with her. It was as if the trees, the grasses, and the flowers released their essence and directed it at her. She burst into tears. Not sad tears. Tears over-flowing with gratitude for what was always present.

"Thank you," she said to the presence of Pax.

"You're welcome," Pax said. "Thank you for being such a graceful expression of a Mother Hen."

Grace smiled, remembering what Pax called her. Yes, it was a title she wanted to keep.

"Yes," Bryan said, answering Johnny's question. "He explained the stones, or at least he told me where they came from."

"And..." Hank demanded. "Where?"

"Crann. They came from Crann. Just like this one."

Bryan held out his hand and showed them the stone Pax had given him.

Rachel clapped her hands over her mouth in surprise. Bryan had said he had something to share but wanted to do it when everyone was present.

"He gave you a stone?" Rachel whispered in delight.

Bryan nodded, his eyes sparkling with tears of happiness.

Hank huffed, impatient with Bryan's roundabout way of getting to the point.

"That's great, Bryan. But what do you mean the stones came from Crann? Who brought them? When? What does it mean?"

Bryan laughed. "Sorry, Hank. Here's the story. It's not long. Pax told it to me quickly because he said he had only a little time."

Hank huffed again, making a hurry-up sign with his hand.

"Well, they didn't actually start at Crann. They ended up in Crann and then came back here."

Seeing Hank's face, Bryan rushed his words.

"Some guy called William Sky found Crann so many generations ago no one knows how long ago it was. He had a stone with him when he climbed the cliff. No. I don't know how he knew how to climb the cliff to Crann, nor does anyone know why he brought a stone from here that first time. Maybe he understood something about stones, or perhaps it was a fluke.

"Pax said that Akotas told him every time the people threw William Sky off the cliff, he brought another stone with him, and he would always leave them on Crann before they threw him off the cliff again."

"They threw him off the cliff nine times?" Rachel asked, thinking of the ten stones that now existed. Nine back at the house, and one in Bryan's hand. If William Sky had one with him the first time, that made nine times being thrown off a cliff. He was definitely persistent. And brave.

"I guess so, and apparently, it was the stones that kept bringing him back to Crann. Pax said that if you leave something in Crann that you have given your heart to, you can return to it."

"He gave his heart to a stone?"

"Yes. He gave each stone memories. Things he loved. Stones keep memories. They carry the history of the world. William Sky brought his memories, his history, and what he loved to Crann and left it there within the stones so he could continue to return. When he left Crann for good, he left two stones and brought eight back.

"Those are the eight given to you by Earl when you all lived in Sandpoint, Idaho. Or I guess Johnny got his when you came here. Earl ended up being the keeper of the stones, or the keeper of William Sky's memories of Crann and Earth.

"Pax said Akotas knew where they kept the stones in Crann because his family had the job of keeping the peace that William Sky brought with him. Akotas brought the stones to Earl during his trips to this world."

"Wait," Evan said, "Akotas traveled between worlds?"

"Apparently," Bryan answered.

"Did you know any of this story?" Evan asked Ava. "You were with Earl. You knew about the package with the stones in it."

"But I didn't know about where the stones came from."

"So, do the stones mean anything now other than bringing us all together?" Grace asked.

Bryan smiled. "Pax didn't know for sure, but he thought that was the purpose, and they tie our two worlds together."

"So Dradon never could have returned to Crann because he left nothing he loved behind. He had no heart to return to?" Grace asked.

Bryan nodded. "That's what Pax told me. Although, of course, they could have brought Dradon back to Crann with them if Pax hadn't dealt with him here. But he couldn't have gone alone."

"But Pax did," Johnny whispered to himself.

Bryan looked over at Johnny before answering. "Yes. He did."

EPILOGUE

Ginny looked out over the crowd gathered around her and not for the first time wondered how it was possible that she was here, doing this, becoming this. Her mother stood beside her, holding her hand, and she could feel the same tremor running through her. It was happening. This magical thing was actually happening.

In front of her, Isira and Akotas stood smiling at her. Akotas smiling the same smile she saw when she looked in the mirror.

The past year had been straight out of a fairy tale. Transported to another world. A father she had never known. People who at first stared at her, then embraced her, and then taught her what she would need to know to face this day.

She had watched her mother bloom and become the woman she had briefly known as a child. Full of life, Maya laughed and danced and spent quiet moments walking with Akotas. Ginny knew her mother was trying to make up for all the years she had wasted. But it was more than that. Akotas had returned for her, but he and Isira would leave soon, and it would be her and her mother who would remain.

Ginny tried not to let fear rise in her. The fear that she would never be capable of being a High Priestess and all that meant. Even though she spent every moment of the last year learning how to guide and lead effectively without using personal power, she worried it wouldn't be enough.

She had spent as much time with Akotas as she could, too. As a teacher, he was a master. As a father, he had waited all these years to be one, and he didn't want to waste a moment of it. They walked and talked and sat by the fire together. Akotas took her into the woods, shared stories of Pax and his childhood and the Decana and Crann history. He tried to condense a lifetime of sharing and teaching into a year. Akotas promised her he had loved her all along and that he would love her into the future. Long after she could no longer see him, he would still be there.

One night he had told her of how he had known the man named Earl Weiland. They were both boys when they met on one of his trips to Ginny's world. They recognized each other immediately. Travelers. Earl from another dimension on Gaia called Erda, and he from Crann.

They called Ginny's world Earth since that is what the people of her world called it, thinking they were the only dimension on the planet Gaia. Both Earl and Akotas thought it ironic that the people called it Earth and yet didn't acknowledge that it was the earth and the nature that grew from and with it that was the true power.

"Never forget that connection, Ginny. Man cannot have power. There is only the connection between all things and the One Intelligence that governs it all. In all worlds, not just this one," Akotas reminded her repeatedly. She promised him she wouldn't. She had seen what happened when it was forgotten.

Akotas was not the only one she had learned from during the past year. Isira taught her the role of being a High Priestess. It would have been something she would have learned through her life if they had lived in Crann, and all of it had to be condensed into a brief span of time.

Once the Decana clan fully understood who Ginny was and what she would become, they taught her, too. She spent days living with different families, learning the small things that they grew up with, and that she didn't know. Isira and Akotas assigned teachers to her who would continue her lessons long after Isira and Akotas. Ceya and Koda would be two of them.

And now this was her day. It was the first time in history where the current High Priestess passed the crown to the next one instead of waiting for their passing. There was no need for a two-moon reprieve. Ginny had a lifetime of knowing the other world. And the people needed to truly accept that she was the legitimate successor in a long line of guardians for peace.

With all the learning she had to do, she had an advantage. She had lived in the other world, and she would not let what happened there happen here in Crann. And she would have help.

Looking out at the crowd surrounding her, Ginny smiled at Bryan and Johnny. Akotas had returned once more to Doveland and invited the two of them to use two stones--the stone he had given Pax, which Pax then gave to Bryan, and the stone that had been in the mirror to be at this ceremony. Bryan knew they would leave these two stones in Crann, where they belonged. The remaining eight stones belonged in their world, their job of bringing their Karass together completed.

Ginny smiled at them, delighted that they were there representing Doveland and the people who had helped her and her mother return to Crann. To her, Bryan and Johnny were Pax's brothers, from another world, but with the same heart.

As she bent forward to accept the wreath of flowers and leaves that Isira was placing on her head, making her the official High Priestess, an owl hooted, and she felt the breath of wind meant only for her. It was like the touch of a cloud--warm, gentle, and reassuring. She knew it was Pax. He had fulfilled his mission. Now, he would always be the peacekeeper, and he would always be at her side.

She and her mother had come home.

• • • ● • ● • • •

The End

Are there parallel worlds? How could there not be? Do we see them and not realize we do? Perhaps. What if we did? Would we accept it as a "reality" or think we have gone crazy?

Maybe the only place we can believe that there is more to life than our five senses report to us is in our dreams. In that way, we expand our perception, and maybe, just maybe, one day, "magical realism" will be part of everyday life.

And it was in a dream that I saw what happens in the prologue of this book. I kept thinking about the dream. Even days later, I could still see that bolt of light and a man rise up from the meadow.

Maya's house was a memory of a house we would walk past on our way to elementary school. We crossed the street and never went there for Halloween, telling ourselves that it was haunted.

Later I imagined that we had missed out by not finding out who lived there. Maybe a woman like Maya with an interesting story to tell.

Pax appeared in a second dream, more of a daydream this time, and I realized he belonged with the first man. However, Pax, as the central character, was a surprise to me. I thought it would be Akotas. But once I realized Pax was the story's pivot, the rest of the story fell into place.

That is the joy of writing. It is trusting in the outcome and going to my computer every day to find out what story these people want to tell me.

Will Bryan and Johnny revisit Crann? Perhaps. But in the meantime, Doveland continues to be, for me, an imaginary town where I would love to live. So visiting it in these books is a joy for me, as I hope it is for you.

And Pax's world? I imagine it is a world where my husband would love to live, or maybe where he came from.

In the meantime, there are always dreams—and books.

Thank you for reading and sharing mine.

You can find all of my books at your favorite book store or on my website: becalewis.com

ACKNOWLEDGEMENTS

I could never write a book without the help of my friends and my book community. Thank you, Jet Tucker, Jamie Lewis, Diana Cormier, and Barbara Budan for taking the time to do the final reader proof. You are a loyal and much-loved reader team. You can't imagine how much I appreciate it.

A huge thank you to Laura Moliter for her fantastic book editing.

Thank you to every other member of my Book Community who helps me make so many decisions that help the book be the best book possible.

Thank you to all the people who tell me that they love to read these stories. Those random comments from friends and strangers are more valuable than gold.

And as always, thank you to my beloved husband, Del, for being my daily sounding board, for putting up with all my questions, my constant need to want to make things better, and for being the love of my life, in more than just this one lifetime.

ALSO BY BECA

The Rivers of Time Series: Women's Lit, Friendship, Small Town, Mystery, Magical Realism, Small Town Fiction
The Returning, The Awakening, The Rising

***Follow Me Here:* Women's Lit, Friendship, Small Town, Mystery, Magical Realism, Small Town Fiction**

The Ruby Sisters Series: Women's Lit, Friendship, Mystery, Small Town Fiction
A Last Gift, After All This Time, And Then She Remembered, As If It Was Real, Almost Innocent

Stories From Doveland: Women's Lit, Friendship, Small Town, Mystery, Magical Realism, Small Town Fiction
Karass, Pragma, Jatismar, Exousia, Stemma, Paragnosis, In-Between, Missing, Out Of Nowhere

The Return To Erda Series: Fantasy
Shatterskin, Deadsweep, Abbadon, The Experiment

The Chronicles of Thamon: Fantasy
Banished, Betrayed, Discovered, Wren's Story

The Shift Series: Spiritual Self-Help
Living in Grace: The Shift to Spiritual Perception
The Daily Shift: Daily Lessons From Love To Money
The 4 Essential Questions: Choosing Spiritually Healthy Habits
The 28 Day Shift To Wealth: A Daily Prosperity Plan
The Intent Course: Say Yes To What Moves You
Imagination Mastery: A Workbook For Shifting Your Reality
Right Thinking: A Thoughtful System for Healing
Perception Mastery: Seven Steps To Lasting Change
Blooming Your Life: How To Experience Consistent Happiness

Perception Parables: Very short stories
Love's Silent Sweet Secret: A Fable About Love
Golden Chains And Silver Cords: A Fable About Letting Go

Advice / Journals
A Woman's ABC's of Life: Lessons in Love, Life, and Career from
Those Who Learned The Hard Way
The Daily Nudge(s): So When Did You First Notice

About Beca

Beca writes books she hopes will change people's perceptions of themselves and the world, and open possibilities to things and ideas that are waiting to be seen and experienced.

At sixteen, Beca founded her own dance studio. Later, she received a Master's Degree in Dance in Choreography from UCLA and founded the Harbinger Dance Theatre, a multimedia dance company, while continuing to run her dance school.

After graduating—to better support her three children—Beca switched to the sales field, where she worked as an employee and independent contractor to many industries, excelling in each while perfecting and teaching her Shift® system, and writing books.

She joined the financial industry in 1983 and became an Associate Vice President of Investments at a major stock brokerage firm, and was a licensed Certified Financial Planner for over twenty years.

This diversity, along with a variety of life challenges, helped fuel the desire to share what she's learned by writing and speaking, hoping it will make a difference in other people's lives.

Beca grew up in State College, PA, with the dream of becoming a dancer and then a writer. She carried that dream forward as she fulfilled a childhood wish by moving to Southern California in 1968. Beca told her family she would never move back to the cold.

After living there for thirty-one years, she met her husband Delbert Lee Piper, Sr., at a retreat in Virginia, and everything changed. They decided to find a place they could call their own, which sent them off traveling around the United States. They lived and worked in a few different places before returning to live in the cold once again near Del's family in a small town in Northeast Ohio, not too far from State College.

When not working and teaching together, they love to visit and play with their combined family of eight children and five grandchildren, read, study, do yoga or taiji, feed birds, and work in their garden.